diary of a 6th grade ninja 3
rise of the red ninjas

BY MARCUS EMERSON
AND NOAH CHILD

ILLUSTRATED BY DAVID LEE

EMERSON PUBLISHING HOUSE

For my parents…

For those of you that don't know me, my name is Chase Cooper, and I'm in sixth grade at Buchanan School. Allow me to fill you in on some details of what's happened since my first diary, but hang on tight 'cause this story starts with a bang.

NORMAL ME | NINJA ME

When I first started Buchanan, the social isolation I *thought* I'd experience never really happened. My cousin Zoe goes here too, so that's been pretty helpful since she already knows everyone. She's popular, though she would never call it that. Instead, I think she'd say she was just friends with everyone. And to be honest, I understand it – she's way cooler than I gave her credit for when we were growing up. Currently, she's the head of the cheerleading squad, first chair violin in Orchestra, the lead in the musical coming up in a few months, and has a perfect 4.0 GPA. Yeah... she's *that* kid.

I think I would consider Brayden my best friend now. I met him on the second day of school during gym class. He's got this weird obsession with werewolves and even introduces himself as a werewolf hunter. But lately his fixation on werewolves has started to bleed over into vampire territory as well. I think at this rate, it'll expand to be an all out "monster" obsession by the end of the school year.

Wyatt, the previous ninja leader, was expelled after stealing money from the student food drive at the beginning of the year. There's been talk that he's returning to Buchanan along with rumors that some had even *seen* him, but nothing has been confirmed. I don't know about that though... how does someone get *un*expelled?

Carlyle, the pirate captain and Wyatt's cousin, went unpunished because he technically didn't do anything wrong. Convincing other students to give him their money so he could win the prize for the Dance 'Til Ya Drop wasn't considered a crime even though it was a shady thing to do. The prize for the dance was that the winner could choose the new mascot of Buchanan. He was going to change the mascot from the Wildcats to the Buccaneers, making his pirate invasion complete, but I stopped him. In doing so, I earned the opportunity to change the mascot myself. I still haven't made a decision yet.

Carlyle also had his classes switched, so we're not longer in any of them together. Can't say I was against the idea. Apparently all it took was his parents to request it, and it was done.

After defeating Wyatt and Carlyle, it's been weird because kids have put me on some kind of pedestal as the hero of Buchanan. Why's it weird? Because I was honestly only doing what I thought was right.

I know what you're probably thinking...

"But Chase, if the school sees you as the hero,

aren't you one of the cool kids now?"

The answer is yes and no. *Yes* as in everyone has an inkling of who I am, but *no* because nobody seems to care much. Honestly, I'd prefer it that way because I get to keep a low profile. *Too much* attention might tip everyone off to my ninja lifestyle.

In the past week, I've also become pretty good friends with a girl named Faith. If you remember in my first diary, there was a moment where everyone was stepping forward admitting guilt in stealing the food drive money. Well, there was a cute red haired girl that did it too – yeah, *that* was *Faith*.

Last week, we were paired together as science lab partners. She's one of the coolest girls I've ever met. She's into *comics*, plays soccer *and* volleyball, *loves* cheesy horror movies from the '90s, *and* has taken *first place* in the annual FPS tournament for *two years* in a row! She was the *only* girl in the tournament and you know what she said after she won?

"Does anyone else hear those bells ringing? Because y'all just got schooled!"

How awesome of a burn is *that?* I mean… y'know, she's cool… for a girl.

Oh, and she doesn't know I'm the leader of a secret ninja clan that trains in the woods during gym class.

I only mention Faith because the first hint of the red ninja uprising came before science class when I was trying to get the nerve to talk to Faith. Although looking back, the appearance of red ninjas should've been

4

obvious. Then again, isn't *everything* obvious when looking back?

"Would you quit messing around and go talk to her?" Zoe snipped.

I poked my head around the corner, pressing my face against the brick wall. Faith's locker was only a few feet away, and it looked like she was almost done with it. "I don't know about this... what if she laughs at me?"

Zoe leaned back, hiding next to me. "Then at least it won't be to your face."

Over the weekend, Zoe convinced me to write a note to Faith telling her that I thought she was cute. Faith was also on the cheerleading squad. Zoe told me Faith started talking about me all the time after we became science lab partners. Pretty cool, huh?

So my cousin came up with this brilliant plan where I would finish the science homework not only for myself, but for Faith as well, and then when I gave her the portion she was going to turn in, I'd also sneak my note in there. She would find it later, and boom... whatever *boom* means. I only hope she checks it before turning it in otherwise the teacher's gonna get an awkward note from a student.

"Okay," I said. "I got this. You're right. She's not even gonna look at the note right now. What'll probably happen is that she'll look at it in science class... which is about five minutes away... and we're lab partners... so what'll *actually* happen is that she'll read the note while I sweat buckets in the seat next to her. *Then* she'll laugh at me. Yeah, this is a *great* idea."

Zoe laughed. "There's only one way to find out!" she yelled as she pushed me into clear view of Faith's locker.

My cousin's shove caught me by surprise, and I stumbled into the hallway, barely missing the other students walking to class. I must've grunted loudly because Faith noticed me right away.

FAITH

"Hey," she said to me.

I stood straight up and tightened a smile. "Huh? Oh, hey, I mean, are you talking to me? *You talkin' to me? I* mean…" I paused long enough to wonder what the *heck* was wrong with me. Did old school ninjas have this much trouble talking to girls? Finally, I let out a sigh. "*Heeeeeey.*"

Faith smiled as she returned her attention to her locker, stacking notebooks at the bottom. "What's up?"

I guffawed like an idiot. "Not much, y'know… the *skyyyyy.*"

At this point I think my brain was *trying* to sabotage me, which was fine because later on I'd just bang my head against a wall. *That'll* show my brain who's boss. Nobody tells me what to do! *Not even my own brain!*

Glancing over her shoulder at me, she giggled. "Nice."

I quickly got to the point. Any more small talk and I think my hair would've fallen out. "So I got all our homework finished, yours *and* mine."

"You finished *both* parts of our homework?" Faith asked, smiling through the few strands of red hair that fell in front of her cheeks.

"Yeah, well I know how stressful it can be to have homework looming over your head," I said blankly, feeling an army of butterflies tearing around in my stomach.

"You can say that again," Faith sighed.

I shook my head and laughed, realizing I had completely zoned out for a moment. *OMG, did I just say something without realizing it?* I took a breath, and with a crack in my voice, I asked, "Say *what* again?"

Faith narrowed her eyes at me as if I were crazy. "That *not* finishing your homework is stressful."

"Ha ha!" I was so relieved about not saying something stupid that I laughed loudly and snorted. Smooth... that's me.

"Thanks for that," Faith said. "I actually completely forgot about it. Lucky too, since it's due in about ten minutes. You're a lifesaver!"

As I pulled my book bag over my shoulder to get Faith's portion of the homework (along with my note), I heard some noise coming from down the hall. I glanced over to see what it was, but because of the flurry of walking students, I couldn't see anything.

"Hey! Watch out!" someone shouted from behind me.

And this is where it gets *crazy*...

Suddenly some kid came out of nowhere and jumped in front of me. He was moving so fast that it looked like a red blur. As he sailed through the air, I felt a tug at my book bag, and before I knew it, the kid had it in his hands.

"Wait!" I shouted. "Give that back!"

Faith fell against her locker with a loud clang. "What just happened? Who *was* that?"

There wasn't time to answer. The kid had my backpack along with the note to Faith *plus* my ninja outfit. I had to take the outfit home to get washed because it was getting a little funky.

Without hesitating, I started running after the backpack thief. It was almost impossible to run at full speed down the hallway because it was packed with other students, and I didn't want to hurt anyone.

I could see the bandit several feet ahead of me. He was wearing a bright red hooded sweatshirt, which made it easy to keep my eyes on him. What thief wears bright red?

The kid turned the corner and glanced back at me, but his hood was up so I couldn't see his face. My bag was swinging wildly as his sneakers squeaked against the linoleum flooring. Then the thief kicked his foot out at the brick wall, flipping himself into the air and *over* another group of students.

Who *was* this guy?

Dragging my hand along the wall, I leaned into it as I rounded the corner. My ninja training came in handy as I took the turn gracefully, hardly losing any speed. What my training *didn't* teach me was how to avoid a collision with a water fountain.

Pain shot through my body as I slammed into the metal tower. I remember spinning in a circle like an ice skater as I fell to the ground. My cheek slapped against the cold floor.

"Hey, man," said a voice from above me. "What's goin' on? What're you running from?"

I looked up. It was Brayden. Wiping the spit off my lip, I started scanning the hallway for the kid in red. "Some noob took my backpack, and I was chasing him down here. Did you see anyone wearing a red hoodie run past you?"

Brayden looked around at the other students walking by. "No," he said. "I didn't see anyone running or anything. They took your backpack?"

I nodded, kicking the metal water fountain. "Yeah. He turned the corner, like, half a second before I became mortal enemies with this fountain."

Brayden turned around, confused. "Serious? I was standing right here the whole time. Nobody in a red hoodie ran by."

Trying to catch my breath, I spoke. "That's

impossible."

"Maybe it was a ghost," Brayden said, excited.

"Right," I replied sarcastically. "A ghost that haunts the hallways of Buchanan School, tormenting students and stealing backpacks. I know that's the first thing I'd do if *I* was a ghost." As I stepped forward, I saw my book bag on the ground. It was leaning against a wall of lockers, open and upside down. Everything in it was spilled on the floor. The students walking to their next class were polite enough to avoid stepping on any of my stuff. "Great."

"Bummer," said Brayden as he started picking my junk up off the ground.

Clenching my jaw, I felt my heart skip a beat – my ninja outfit! Dropping to my knees, I quickly grabbed the bag and reached my hand inside of it. Frantically, I scraped my fingers along the canvas, but found nothing.

It was completely empty.

Brayden tapped a stack of papers on the floor to even them out. "You didn't see who it was?"

I looked over my shoulder at the other students, hoping to see a red sweatshirt in the crowd. I never did. "No. I didn't see his face. He just appeared out of nowhere too. I mean, one minute I was standing there talking to Faith, and then the next minute..." This time it felt like my heart completely stopped. "...*Faith*."

Brayden squinted an eye at me. "One minute you were talking to Faith, and then the next minute *Faith*? Is Faith another word for something? Because you just lost me."

Panic stricken, I searched through all of my papers on the floor, throwing them out of the way. "Where is it? *Where is it?*"

"Where's *what*, dude?" Brayden asked. "Now you're just freakin' me out."

"My science homework!" I squealed. "There was something I had with my science homework that…" I finally checked the last sheet of paper on the floor. Faith's note was gone. "Gah!" I shouted as I whipped my science textbook across the floor.

"What is it?"

I didn't have the nerve to tell Brayden about the note so I didn't. "My ninja outfit was in my bag! It's gone," I said, raising my eyebrows. "That kid *took* it."

Just then, the bell rang, signaling the start of fifth period.

"I'll catch you after class," said Brayden. We didn't have fifth period together. "We'll figure out who that kid was, okay?"

I tightened my lips into a fake smile. The knot in my stomach twisted a little more. "Sure, after class."

The hallways of Buchanan were suddenly silent. I could hear the sound of doors shutting as classes started. Picking up the rest of my stuff, I shoved it all into my bag and headed to fifth period… *science class.*

Monday. 12:07 PM. Science class.

"Chase, you're late," Mrs. Olsen said, standing at the front of the room.

"Sorry," I said quietly. She was usually pretty cool if you simply apologized instead of making an excuse.

She pressed her lips together and nodded. "Mm hmm. Just have a seat, and we'll get started."

I set my bag on the long black desk. Faith was already there with her textbook out. Zoe and her friend Emily were in the desk behind us. I took my seat and scooted a few inches away from Faith – I don't know why exactly. Maybe I'm shyer than I care to admit?

"I was beginning to think you were gonna skip!" Faith joked.

Zoe leaned forward. "Yeah right, this guy?" she whispered, aiming her thumb at me. "He's way too chicken to do something like that!"

Pulling out my chair, I ignored Zoe's comment and took a seat.

Faith leaned closer and whispered quietly. "Good to see you have your bag back."

"Back?" Zoe asked from behind. "Where'd it go?"

Faith turned slightly, only enough that she could make eye contact with my cousin. "Some kid ran off with it right after lunch!" Then she turned toward me. "That's why you were late, huh?"

I nodded, setting my science book on the desk. "Yeah, I chased the kid, but didn't catch him. Lucky for me, he dropped my bag, but not before dumping it out on the floor."

"You mean this happened within the last ten or so minutes? *After* I pushed you... I mean, after you made your *own* decision to *step* into the hallway?" Zoe asked, concerned. "I hope it wasn't before... *you know.*"

"Before what?" Faith asked.

"Nothing!" I said hotly. "Before *nothing.*"

Zoe understood as she folded her hands on her desk. I think she could tell that Faith was going to ask more questions so she quickly changed the subject. "And you didn't pull any... *ninja* moves on him?"

Emily snickered.

I shot a look at Zoe with my eyes wide open. My brain was screaming for her to stay quiet, but on the outside, all I could do was blink in Morse code – it'd probably help if I *knew* Morse code.

Faith LOL'd. "Yeah, right. Didja ninja-kick him in

14

the face?"

"No," I said. "Ninjas don't really do that."

"Are you sure?" Zoe asked. "I'm pretty sure ninjas kick faces. It'd be disappointing if they didn't. I mean, all that training just to *not* face-kick a dude?"

Zoe had a way of taking a joke right to the line, and then stepping past it, but it was always in a way that made me chuckle.

Zoe continued. "Oh, by the way, my dad can drive us to the skate party on Friday."

I nodded, trying my best to look uninterested because cool guys are always uninterested. "Cool."

"Your sister's riding with us too," Zoe added.

I leaned back in my chair and sighed. "I forgot my third grade lamewad sister was coming too."

"Hey," Zoe snipped. "Your sister's awesome, so shut it."

"*Awesome* isn't the word I'd use to describe her," I replied.

"Well, it's an all-school skating party so it's not like you can keep her out," Zoe said.

"You're right," I replied. "But I *can* decide to stay home."

Zoe squinted her eyes and sneered. "Like I'd let you sit this one out!"

Faith glanced at my book bag and furrowed her brow. "Did they take anything?"

Mrs. Olsen interrupted our conversation. "Excuse me," she said, standing over our desk. "When you four are finished, would you mind turning in your homework?"

"Right," Emily said, passing a couple sheets of paper to Faith.

Faith looked at me. "Where's our homework?"

I took a breath, and shook my head. "That's the thing that kid took."

Faith paused. "Are you serious? He took our homework?"

"Is there a problem?" Mrs. Olsen asked, hovering over our desk. "Pass your assignments up front."

"I don't..." I said. "I don't have it."

Mrs. Olsen didn't skip a beat, probably because her heart was hardened from years of miserable students failing to turn in assignments. It almost looked like she enjoyed it. "That's unfortunate. Faith, you know that this was a co-op assignment so yours is also considered late."

Faith nodded, remaining silent.

The rest of science was awkward. Faith never came out and told me she was angry, but I could tell from her short sentence responses to anything I said. The only thing that could fix this was if I found the thief before the day was out. Maybe Mrs. Olsen would be cool if I brought it in after school and just apologized instead of making excuses.

Yeah, right… and maybe someday I'll live on Mars.

Monday. 2:45 PM. The end of the school day.

The rest of the day was pretty uneventful. After school, I met up with Brayden so we could look for the kid in the red hooded sweatshirt, but we had no luck. Even Zoe got in on the hunt, checking out the girl's restrooms, in case it was a girl in the hoodie. She never found anything.

As the students gathered in the front lobby of Buchanan, they filtered through the doors, excited to leave for home. Kids laughed and shouted at each other, celebrating the end of the day. At this point, everyone was in a good mood since school was out.

Everyone except for me.

"Maybe we should call it a day?" Brayden asked, standing on a bench, searching for the kid in red.

A random student passed by me laughing. "Hey, lover boy, whatcha up to?"

Their friend laughed too, and then I realized it was *me* they were laughing at.

I grunted at them like a confused ape. "Huh?"

They continued walking down the hallway laughing.

"What was that?" I asked.

Brayden threw his arms into the air. "Who cares? Can we just go home now?"

I was already frustrated, and the thought of giving up made it worse. "Come on! You're a werewolf hunter, right? Why don't you make some use of your hunting skills and *find* this kid?"

Brayden folded his arms. "Aren't you supposed to be some kind of ninja? Why didn't you use your ninja skills in the first place to prevent this from happening? I think a ninja-kick to the face would've been effective!"

"*See?*" Zoe asked, smiling. "A ninja-kick to the face! I'm not the only one who thinks that's a thing!"

"Besides,' Brayden continued. "Werewolf hunting is an art. It takes patience and skill." He paused. "Looks like you won't be able to turn in your science homework today after all."

I curled my lip and shook my head, frustrated.

I noticed a small group of girls giggling at me as they passed by. A few of them even pointed. Turning around, I checked to see if there was some kind of joke behind me that I wasn't aware of, but there wasn't. They *were* pointing at me."

"Um, Chase?" Zoe said from down the hall. "You

19

might want to come over here and see this."

Brayden and I jogged down the hallway, to where Zoe was standing, staring at the brick wall. As I approached, I could see that she was staring at a sheet of paper that was taped up. One look and I recognized it immediately.

It was the note I wrote to Faith.

Hey Faith,
I know we just met, but I think you're pretty cute!!!!!!!!!!!!!!!!! I look forward to hearing your response! That is all.
- Chase Cooper (your science lab partner)

"Whoops," Zoe said. "That can't be a good thing."
"Look forward to hearing your response?" Brayden

asked. "Were you looking at a job application when you wrote this?"

"Funny," I said, upset.

Brayden made a disgusted look with his face. "Why so many exclamation points?"

"Because, dude," I said. "More exclamation points means I'm more serious!"

"No," Zoe sighed, shaking her head. "It just makes it look like you don't understand grammar."

"Whatever, *you* helped me write it," I said to my cousin.

She put a hand on her hip and leaned into it with attitude. "When I left, there was only one exclamation point. You added the other fourteen when I wasn't looking."

Like the brilliant comeback king I am, I tried to keep my reply classy. "*Nuh-uh.*"

Glancing down the hallway, I saw several sheets of paper taped to the walls. They were all copies of my note to Faith... *hundreds* of them. I spun in place and looked at the lobby of the school where we had just come from. The copies of the note were plastered there as well.

"How did we miss these?" Zoe asked.

I shook my head. "We were so focused on finding the kid in red that we didn't even notice these." I scanned down the hallway leading to the opposite end of the school. The note was taped up everywhere. "It's gonna be a rough day tomorrow."

Tuesday. 7:30 AM. Before homeroom.

It was one of the few times I was the first one in the room. I tried my best to fake being sick so I could stay home, but Mom saw right through it. It was too embarrassing to tell her the truth, so instead I convinced her to bring me here early. That way I could at least avoid students before school started. My plan was to steer clear of everyone for the rest of the day, although I didn't know how.

Brayden and Zoe stayed after school to help take down the copies of my note. Even Principal Davis and Mr. Cooper came out and helped. Mr. Davis questioned me on how it happened, so I told him everything. He said he was going to get to the bottom of it, but I told him to leave it alone for now. It was already enough attention that the note was out there, but I think launching an investigation would've just made it worse. With any luck, this whole thing would blow over in a day or two, but with my track record, it was probably going to *blow up* in my face.

I sat silently for the next fifteen minutes, watching the other students enter through the door. I could hear the hushed whispers coming from various groups in the room as they peeked out at me.

Whatever. I had other fish to fry... like, *who* was the kid in the red hooded sweatshirt? He came out of nowhere, and when he grabbed my bag, I could feel how strong he was. He basically *ripped* the bag from my hands. But that's assuming it was a *boy*. It could've easily been a *girl* – the way she gracefully weaved in and out of students as I chased after her, and then performed that Olympic-styled back flip to avoid an accident? I don't know about you, but I don't know any boys who can do that.

Unless they were ninjas...

"Chase," said Zoe's voice as she entered the room. She took the seat in front of me and turned around, setting a stack of paper down on my desk. "These are copies of your note that I've already taken down just *this morning.*"

My stomach turned as I stared at the stack of paper. "Did you see who was putting them up?"

Zoe shook her head. "I asked around, and nobody else did either. Whoever's doing it is pretty good at sneaking around."

"Good? They're *great* at it," I said, putting the

copies of my note into my book bag. I didn't want to set them in the garbage can because they'd probably find their way back onto the walls if I did. "These weren't on the walls when I got to school this morning. I got here around 7:25 and it's almost 7:45. That means whoever it was had about twenty minutes to do it."

"*One kid* couldn't do all *that* though, could they?" Zoe asked.

I shrugged my shoulders. "You'd be surprised."

Zoe smiled, trying to lighten the mood with her sense of humor. "At least you signed your first *and* last name, right?"

"You told me I should!" I whispered angrily. "Just to make sure Faith knew *exactly* who it was from! Well, I hope you're happy 'cause now the whole *school* knows!"

Zoe frowned. I felt bad for chewing her out, but I was too angry to take it back. Not at her, but angry at the fact that a stupid note had the power to destroy what little social life I actually had. Maybe I could run away to South America or something. I hear they still have tribes that are completely void of technology.

But instead of an apology from me, it came from her.

"I'm sorry," she whispered as she turned in her seat. "I shouldn't have pushed you..."

"Zoe..." I replied, but still felt hot headed. I didn't say anything after her name.

The students in the room were still giggling and pointing at me. Some of the bigger kids shouted some insults – lover boy, cupid, heartbreaker… the usual uncreative things kids say when they're mean.

"I don't know how this could possibly get any worse," Zoe said.

"Allow me to show you then," said a voice from the door. It was Brayden. He took the seat next to us, but not before setting another sheet of paper down on my desk.

Without looking at the paper, I spoke. "We *know*. My note is all over the school again."

Brayden shook his head. "Look at the paper."

When I looked down, I felt the air escape from my lungs. It was a copy of the school newspaper that had been printed overnight. On the front page of the single sheet of paper was a photo of a kid in a ninja outfit. Though everyone in my ninja clan had similar outfits, we could always tell which ones were ours. And the one in the photo was definitely *mine*.

Things had officially gotten *worse*.

In the photo, the ninja was carrying a laptop and running from hall monitors. The bold title across the front page said, *"Wanted For Stealing: The Buchanan Ninja."*

"Are you serious?" I whispered.

At that moment, the bell rang. Before it was even finished, two hall monitors entered the room and marched to the front of the class. A taller boy wearing aviator glasses accompanied them. When they reached the front of the room, Mrs. Robinson stood from her desk and started speaking.

"Children," she said. "It seems we have a bit of a

situation at Buchanan School. Yesterday, a few students witnessed what they thought was a child running around in a ninja costume, stealing things."

"I'll take it from here," said the boy with aviator glasses. He turned toward the class and removed the overly large sunglasses from his face. I recognized him from walking the hallways, but I had never actually spoken to him. He made a smile that was obviously fake. "The name's Gavin. Some of you might recognize me, as I'm the captain of the hall monitors. What your homeroom teacher has said is true – there's a ninja runnin' around here creating all sorts of headaches for me and my team."

A student at the front of the class raised their hand. "Do you know who it is?"

Zoe glanced back at me, worried.

"Unfortunately at this time, we have no leads as to *who* the ninja is," Gavin said. "Which is why we're going from classroom to classroom askin' if anyone has seen anything."

I sunk in my chair and folded my arms, trying my best to blend in with the plastic desk. Shutting my eyes, I listened to Gavin continue talking like some sort of cowboy.

"Any of you bear witness to suspicious activity lately?" Gavin asked.

Nobody answered.

The captain of the hall monitors sighed as he nodded and returned his sunglasses to his face. "Welp, ya'll will be happy to know that Buchanan's president has given us the go ahead to do *everything* within our power to make sure we find this kid. It's pretty safe to say that anyone who's an accomplice will likely get what's comin' to them as well. We'd like to have this case wrapped up before the skate party on Friday night."

Oh wonderful. Now the school president is involved. Not only am *I* at risk of getting busted, but all my closest friends are too! This is *not* my best year ever.

Gavin and the two hall monitors nodded at Mrs. Robinson and left the room without saying another word. She stood at the front of the class and continued the announcements.

"I think we could all use a bit of good news today, don't you?" she asked the class. "Which is why I'm proud to say that the totals for the food drive from the beginning of the year have come in, *and...* Buchanan made well over ten thousand dollars."

The students gasped and then cheered loudly as they screamed together. *"Class trip!"*

"That's correct," Mrs. Robinson said. "And the location was decided upon just yesterday. We'll be going to Adventure Caves at the end of the year."

It was as if everyone had lost their minds. Kids jumped from their desk and screamed like the old people on the game show my parents watch in the morning. They were going nuts! Even Zoe was hopping around her desk and laughing with her friends. I glanced over at Brayden... was he wiping a *tear* from his cheek?

"Adventure Caves..." Brayden said as he looked at me with wet eyes. "Is the most awesome place in the universe." Then he spoke so softly that I couldn't hear him over the shouts of other students, but I could read his lips. "I'm *so* happy!"

Watching everyone celebrate, I felt a little jealous that I didn't feel the same excitement as they did. The kid in the red hooded sweatshirt weighed heavily on my mind, and no matter how hard I tried, I couldn't stop thinking about him.

Zoe took her seat again and smiled at me. Realizing I wasn't jumping up and down like a maniac, her face sobered up. "I'm sorry. This is just really great news."

"No, it's fine," I replied. "I get it. I wish I could be happy too."

She put her hands on my desk and leaned closer. "We'll find this kid, okay? The one running around in the ninja costume."

I was surprised. "You mean you don't think it was me?"

Zoe shook her head. "Of course not, I mean... *was it?*"

"No!"

"Good," she said, relieved. "That would've made Sunday brunches between our families weird. So what do you think? Do you *know* who it was?"

"When that kid snatched my bag yesterday, he took my ninja outfit," I explained to my cousin. "I think it's the same kid who's plastering my stupid love notes all over the school."

Zoe nodded.

"That makes things easier, doesn't it?" Brayden asked, wiping the last of his happy tears from his face. "At least you're not looking for *two* different people."

"Carlyle, maybe?" Zoe asked. "Could he be out to get you again?"

"No," I replied. "The kid in the red hoodie was shorter than him."

Brayden said what was on the back of my mind. "Wyatt?"

Zoe sat up and shook her head angrily. "No way. He was expelled from Buchanan. You can't come back from something like that."

"But Carlyle said he was returning someday," Brayden said. "And people have said they've *seen* him walking around."

"Yeah?" Zoe asked. "Which people?"

Brayden paused. "Friends... of some friends."

"Exactly," Zoe said folding her arms. "It's just a bunch of rumors. Tell me one instance where someone can comeback with no consequences."

"Video games," I said. "People die and respawn in games *all* the time."

"*Seriously?*" Zoe asked. "You're going to use video games in your defense?"

I did my best to keep a straight face. Some of my best ninja training came from video games, but I didn't want to say that. Finally, I shrugged it off. "It was just a joke."

Tuesday. 10:40 AM. Gym class.

I spent the two periods after homeroom in a funk. Zoe and Brayden were doing their best to cheer me up, but with the rest of the school poking fun at my note, it wasn't an easy task for them. At least they were trying, and that felt good.

Since my ninja outfit had been stolen by the kid in red, I had to attend my ninja clan meeting in my street clothes. It probably wasn't a big deal to anybody, but it was to me.

I decided it was too dangerous for the ninja clan to train anymore, at least for the next few days. We were good, but I was afraid that Gavin and his hall monitors might be *gooder*... I mean, *better*. If anyone else got busted, I'd feel terrible, but it's not only that. If anyone else gets busted, then the entire ninja operation becomes compromised, and it would only be a matter of time

31

before they pinned the theft from the school paper on me since it was *my* ninja outfit.

It wasn't an easy decision, but I felt it would be best if I tried to handle this on my own. I know the other ninjas would do everything they could to help, but it was too risky. Plus if it was just me, I felt I'd have better control of the situation.

When I stepped into the wooded area where we train, the rest of the ninja clan was waiting for me.

"Sir, your ninja robes," one of the shorter ninjas said. "Have you misplaced them again?"

He was referring to when I gave Carlyle my robes in defeat last month. "No," I answered. "They were stolen from me yesterday."

There were some smart members of my clan, and one of them spoke up, understanding before I even explained it. "So that *wasn't* you in the school photo!"

I nodded.

Everyone sighed out of relief at the same time. I'm pretty sure the leaves on the trees shook because of the sudden gust of breath.

"Then we must find this kid," said the short ninja. His voice suddenly grew raspy as he clenched his fists. "And we must make him *cry* like a little *baby*."

"No," I said immediately. "Remember? We don't *hurt* people."

The short ninja lowered his head, embarrassed. "You're right. I am sorry."

One of the taller ninjas stepped forward and removed his mask. It was Brayden. After defeating Carlyle last month, I told him he could join my ninja clan if he still wanted to. He jumped at the chance. "So what can we do then?" he asked.

I sighed, placing my hands on my hips. "The rest of you are going to lay low for the week. No training or anything. Don't change into your outfits and *don't* try to find the other kid who has *my* outfit."

"But that's crazy," Brayden said boldly.

I shrugged my shoulders. "It's for the best. Things are just too hot right now."

"Like your crush on Faith?" one of the ninjas in the back giggled.

I remained silent, allowing the ninja time to laugh at their own joke. I can't believe the teasing had even made it into my ninja clan. I didn't want to yell at the ninja though because I if I were him, I probably would've made the same comment.

Discouraged, the other ninjas changed back into their street clothes behind the trees. Not another word was said as they left the hideout. It wasn't my proudest moment, but I felt excited about investigating on my own. Like I'd become a superhero detective, but without the "superhero."

Brayden switched back into his street clothes and stayed behind as the last of my ninja clan left.

"You know I can't let you do this on your own, right?" Brayden asked.

He really *was* a good friend. "I know."

Brayden took a seat on the trunk of a fallen tree. "How 'bout that Gavin kid? Somethin's a little off about him, right?"

I laughed.

"It's like he was plucked straight from one of my dad's cowboy movies!" Brayden said.

I sat on the log next to my friend, the werewolf hunter. "Yeah, but that doesn't mean he's not good at what he does."

"He's got the school president's approval to do whatever it takes to find the ninja," Brayden sighed. "It's a short list of suspects that's eventually going to end with you."

I nodded but didn't say anything.

"So if this kid is pretending to be a ninja, then the question is..." Brayden paused. "How do we catch a ninja?"

"A ninja only gets caught if he wants to get

caught," I replied. "Otherwise they're not very good."

"Here's a thought – we're assuming this kid in the red hoodie *isn't* a ninja," Brayden said. "But what if he is?"

"I trust every single kid in my ninja clan," I said, slightly upset. "None of them would try to frame me like that."

"Sure, the ninjas in *your* clan would never betray you," Brayden explained. "But what about the ninjas from when *Wyatt* was in charge?"

Immediately, I felt like an idiot. It was possible that Brayden was right.

"A lot of those ninjas probably didn't keep being a ninja after you had him booted from the school, right?"

"Right," I said. "Mostly the tough ones who just wanted to fight and stuff."

"*Exactly*," Brayden said, pointing his finger at me. "So yeah, that's a possibility."

I stood from the log and hopped on top of it. With the other ninjas gone from the hideout, it was easier to train since I wasn't worried about slipping up in front of them.

Brayden stood and stepped aside, allowing me the entire log to train on. "Still have problems with balance?"

It wasn't a secret that my ability to balance was terrible. For some reason I just can't stand on one foot for too long. Maybe it has something to do with my low center of gravity, or maybe I'm cursed.

My dad made me watch one of his *super boring*

ancient karate movies once where this kid was taught martial arts by a short handy man or something. The kid in the movie had to practice the crane stance where he would have to balance on one leg while keeping the other one propped in the air. Then he would raise his hands over his head like they were the crane's wings or something, I dunno. I've been using that technique in my ninja training to hopefully get better at balancing. So far, it hasn't been working.

"I think I'm destined to stand on two feet forever," I sighed.

"Could be worse," Brayden replied.

We spent the rest of gym class showing each other new sweet ninja moves we learned from the Internet.

Tuesday. 11:55 AM. Right after lunch.

Once I entered the lunchroom, it was obvious that everyone was staring and making fun of me.

Copies of my note to Faith were hanging all over the cafeteria walls. The teachers did their best to remove them, but whoever was putting them up moved faster than they did.

It was awful, it really was. I found the only empty table at the far end of the room and took a seat, realizing it was empty for a reason. The wood on the bench was warped and felt wet. The surface of the table was cracked and coming apart. Why they hadn't thrown the table away yet was beyond me.

Have you ever had to eat lunch by yourself in a roomful of kids as they talked about you? It's not something I would wish upon my worst enemy, which was the kid in red at the moment.

Seriously, you're at a huge table in the corner by yourself, and whether people are looking at you or not, you *think* they are. So that makes you aware of every single move you make. Am I chewing my food weird? Is my shirt bunching up in the back? Am I blinking too fast? It's maddening!

With five minutes left on the clock, I decided to stand out in the lobby and wait for the bell to ring. The cafeteria walls were tinted glass so it wasn't like I was hiding or anything, but I still did my best to ignore everyone, turning toward the doors of the school and staring outside.

And then I saw him out of the corner of my eye. It was the kid in the red hoodie, standing in the middle of the hallway that led to the east end of the school. He was taping another copy of my note to the lockers, but hadn't noticed me yet.

"Hey!" I shouted without thinking.

The kid looked at me, but his hood was over his face so I still couldn't see who it was. He sprang back from the locker and sprinted down the hall.

I immediately started chasing after him. Pulling my book bag tighter around my shoulders, I ran as fast as I could.

"Stop!" I cried. "You're finished! I saw you put that poster up! You're probably the same guy that caused trouble while wearing my ninja outfit!"

The thief looked over his shoulder at me, and then started running even faster. It was everything I could do to keep up. As long as I kept him in my sight, I knew it was only a matter of time before he ran into another teacher walking the halls.

He turned the corner and fled down the same

corridor he disappeared in the day before. Without any students, he moved like a bullet. I was still a good twenty feet behind him, but I could see him reach into his sweatshirt pocket and pull out a small bag. Then he threw it at his feet as hard as he could.

There was a small "poof" sound as the hallway filled with chalk dust. The kid had used some sort of diversion tactic! The dust was thick enough that it was difficult to see through, but I still went in at full speed.

When I emerged from the cloud on the other side, the kid in the red hoodie had disappeared.

"Crumb!" I shouted, shaking the white dust off my clothing.

I knelt on the floor to inspect the smoke bomb he threw. It was crudely built, but *clever* – just a small mesh sack with a string around the top, probably loose enough that when it was thrown at the ground, the whole thing would blast out into a cloud. It was the sort of thing a ninja would carry around with them.

Sighing, I stood up and looked at the classroom doors down the hall. They were all closed shut, and probably locked since it was lunchtime. The chase had led me to the science wing of the school, to where my next class was going to be.

Suddenly, I heard the click sound of a door shutting. I snapped my attention at each door down the hallway, watching carefully for any kind of movement. The click sound came again, this time of someone turning a *lock*. I instantly knew which door it was and ran to it.

Turning the handle, I shouted. "I know you're in there! You're trapped now so there's nothing you can do!"

The rectangular glass on the door was dark because the lights in the room were off.

I tried the handle again. "Open the door! There's nowhere to—"

The bell rang over my shouting. Students began filling the hallway as I stood in place in front of the locked door. That's fine, I thought. I'll just wait until the teacher came and unlocked it, which happened to be at that exact moment.

"Good afternoon, Chase," said Mr. Lien. "Ya little heartbreaker."

Really?? Even Mr. Lien was going to poke fun at me??

I nodded once and stepped out of the way. "Mr. Lien."

The teacher slid his key into the door and turned the lock. "Something I can help you with, son?"

I hated when adults called me "son." I shook my head. "No, I just thought I saw something weird in the window of your classroom. I thought I'd wait until you unlocked it to see what it was."

"Oh," Mr. Lien replied as he swung the door open and flipped the light switch. "Well, have a look around. Let me know if what you find is as weird as you thought it was!"

Tossing a thumbs-up into the air, I replied. "Roger

roger!"

I jumped into the room, ready to confront the kid in the red hoodie, but to my surprise, he wasn't there. In fact, there wasn't a single other person in the room when I looked around.

This kid, no… this *ninja*… had skills.

Tuesday. 12:05 PM. Science class
(like, 10 minutes later).

At this point in the day, I wasn't really surprised that things kept getting worse…

"I want a new lab partner," was the first thing Faith said when she sat down.

I had done a good job of avoiding her out of embarrassment the entire day up until now. Obviously she was my lab partner so there was no getting around that. I wasn't sure what her reaction to my note was going to be, but I guess I hoped it was going to be good.

"What?" I asked, confused.

She looked at me with soft puffy eyes. I think she had been crying. "I want a new lab partner," she repeated.

I sighed, nodding. "Because of that stupid note?"

"Yeah," she whispered. "Because of that stupid note."

43

I made eye contact with Zoe, who was sitting behind us. She tightened a sad smile, but said nothing.

Raising my eyebrows, I spoke. "You have no idea how hard today has been for me. It's like a gauntlet of insults every time I go *anywhere* in this school."

"How hard it's been for *you?*" she whispered, harsher than I expected.

"Yeah," I replied, offended by her answer. "It was a note from *me*. If anything I just gave you ammunition to poke fun at me with your friends!"

"You think this has been a good time for *me?*" Faith sneered. "That little love note was from *you* to *me*. There are like, five other girls named Faith in this school, and if you would've just signed the name 'Chase,' then nobody would know for sure who you were referring to, but *thank God* you added *'your science lab partner'* so there wasn't any doubt in who the note was addressed to! Pretty sure I'm the only *'Faith'* at Buchanan with a science lab partner named *'Chase.'*"

In situations like this, I get defensive rather than apologetic. "So what's your *point? I'm* the one getting made fun of, not *you!*"

Faith dropped her jaw, shocked. Then she spoke *loudly*. "You think you're the only one affected?"

"*Oh yeah, well—,*" I started to answer with a witty comeback that would completely shut her down, but she interrupted me.

"Kids are calling me your *wife*," she snipped. "They ask how our *relationship* is going, and when our *wedding* date is. They ask if we have names chosen for our *kids* yet and if I've been practicing my signature with *'Cooper'* as my last name! They suggest things like starting a *joint banking account* with you, but not before getting you to sign a prenuptial agreement!" She threw her hands out, and yelled, *"I don't even know what that means!"*

My brain froze up, and like the stupid boy I am, I said, *"So?"*

She replied instantly. "I *hate* you!"

And there it was. The circuits in my brain completely fried and I just stared at her, doing my best to show no emotion. Ninjas probably never showed emotion, but that was really difficult for *this* ninja.

Finally, I blinked and looked around the room. *Everyone*, including the *teacher*, was staring at us. Our conversation had started with whispers, but ended with all out shouting.

Someone from the back of the class broke the silence. *"Looks like they might break up, you guys!"*

Everyone laughed, but I think that was the straw that broke the camel's back. Faith grabbed her book bag and ran out the door. I sat in place, knowing that if I ran after her, the kids would probably shout about that too. How badly I wished I actually knew how to vanish like a ninja at that moment.

I don't know where Faith went, but she didn't return to class that day. In fact, I didn't see her at all for the rest of the school day. Most likely, she went home.

Wednesday. 7:45 AM. Homeroom.

When I got to Buchanan the next morning, I was back to my *normal "kind-of-late-for-school"* routine. I'm happy to say that the copies of my note weren't hung in every single hallway like it had been for the last day and half, but a few of them still lingered. Earlier, when I opened my locker, some even fell out. Apparently somebody thought it would be funny to slip them in there.

Zoe hadn't said much during science the day before, but given the night to think it over, she did her typical *"I'm-just-trying-to-help"* thing.

"I talked to Faith last night," she said as she took her seat.

I didn't look at her. "I don't care."

"*That's* the problem, isn't it?" she asked.

As the bell rang, Mrs. Robinson stood at the front

of the class and performed the daily ritual of spouting off announcements. I zoned out for half of them up until she mentioned the skate party. "…and don't forget the skate party on Friday. It goes from 5-7 PM, and if you've got your own skates, you can bring those too. Since it's an all school skate party, Buchanan is providing pizza for dinner, so don't forget that you'll need an extra two dollars if you'd like to eat."

My attention shifted back to my cousin in front of me. "Why's that the problem?"

"Because you think you're the only one affected by this whole thing," Zoe whispered without turning around.

"If I remember correctly, *you* were the one that convinced me to write the note in the first place," I replied.

"Right, but I've already apologized for that," Zoe said. "What's done is done, but you didn't have to talk to Faith like that yesterday."

"I didn't talk to her like *anything*," I snipped.

Zoe grunted. "You're *such* a boy! I called her last night to see if she was alright."

I paused. "What'd she say?"

"Oh, so *now* you care?" Zoe asked.

When I didn't answer, she turned around. "Faith isn't as angry as you think she is. She's more upset with everyone making fun of her."

"If I could stop it, I would," I said.

Zoe shook her head. "It didn't sound like she cared though. She knows this will all blow over, and I think you should know that too."

Easy for Zoe to say since it wasn't happening to her, right? I just nodded my head. She turned around, and didn't say anything for the rest of homeroom.

Wednesday. 10:35 AM. Gym class.

Standing against the brick walls, I waited for Brayden to exit the locker room. Zoe was already talking with her group of friends as they tossed a volleyball around. Mr. Cooper was taking attendance in his usual uncaring way, checking student's names off on his clipboard.

"What's up, man?" Brayden asked as he joined me on the wall.

"Nothing," I said. "Can't wait to get outside and work on my balance. All this stress over the past couple days really has me in a twist. Maybe standing on one leg for an hour will help me work it off."

"Right?" Brayden said. "Isn't it ironic that we're getting *real* exercise during gym class?"

I laughed. Ah, how it felt good to laugh again.

Brayden pointed at the gym teacher. "You know I

just realized you have the same last name as Mr. Cooper."

I nodded. "Yeah. Cooper is a pretty common last name. What would be crazy would be if *he* had the same *first* name as me too!"

Brayden looked like a confused dog. "What name would that be?"

I stared at my friend, waiting for the joke to catch up with him.

Finally, he slapped his forehead. "Oh right. *Chase. Chase* is your first name."

I patted him on the shoulder and looked at the other students in the gym.

"At least nobody's making fun of you in here about that note," Brayden said, reminding me that I should feel terrible.

"Give it time. At some point in class, someone will say *something*."

As if to prove me right, I heard someone shout loud enough that it echoed off the walls. "*They name you 'Chase' because you're always 'chasing' after girls?*"

Mr. Cooper lowered the clipboard, and pointed at the student who shouted. "That's it. Get your stuff out of the locker room and walk directly to detention!" he said angrily. "Do *not* pass 'go.' Do *not* collect two hundred dollars!"

I smiled as I watched the kid get flustered. He didn't argue with Mr. Cooper though. Nobody ever did. The gym teacher looked back at me and nodded once. He didn't say anything, but he didn't have to.

Mr. Cooper turned to the center of the gym and spoke. "Volleyball inside, flag football outside! To anyone walking the track; do it carefully! Maintenance is clearing out the wooded area down there so there's some heavy machinery driving around. Stay *on* the track, and you'll be fine!"

"What?" I asked. "Clearing out the wooded area?"

Mr. Cooper returned his attention to his clipboard and started scribbling notes. "Yep. Seems as if Gavin and his crew found a hidden spot back there with some lockers and ninja costumes. He convinced the school president that it should be torn up."

I felt sick, and I could see that Brayden did too. Our ninja hideout was discovered and probably being ripped to shreds at that exact moment. "And Principal Davis just *allowed* that to happen? How much power does the school president *have?*"

"It's not about how much power he has," Mr. Cooper said shaking his head. "It's about the fact that this school has wanted to extend the track and field for years, but those woods have always been in the way. Principal Davis finally has his reason to clear them out, what with the psycho in the ninja outfit causing trouble and all."

"But that was *one* kid!" I said, feeling short of breath.

Mr. Cooper paused. "I saw the hidden area myself this morning. It looked like dozens of kids have been messing around back there for a *long* time. There was even an abandoned locker *filled* with black ninja costumes… you don't know anything about that, do you?"

"No," I answered immediately, looking away.

"Good," Mr. Cooper said as he pushed the door to the gymnasium open. "Because it seems like they'd be a bad group of kids to get involved with."

Brayden and I followed the line of students out the door. As soon as we got outside, I could hear the sound of chainsaws and tractors working at a distance. When we finally reached the track, we saw what Mr. Cooper was talking about.

The trees were already mostly chopped down. The hideout was completely demolished and exposed. It was weird seeing the sunlight pour across the entire area because I had only seen it covered in shadows. The old rusty lockers had been pulled away from the woods and were sitting out in the open next to some unmanned porta-potties. Stuffed in a metal trashcan next to the lockers were the black ninja robes of my clan.

I made eye contact with one of the students walking closest to me. It was another member of my ninja clan, but dressed in his street clothes. The sadness I saw in his eyes was heavy.

"This isn't your fault," Brayden said as he walked next to me on the track.

Another student, a girl, caught up with us. "We'll find who did this, sir. We'll make them pay."

But I was too emotionally exhausted to feel *anything*. "Just forget it," I said. "It's over. This whole thing is done, and it's not worth fighting about."

"But, sir," the girl said.

"No," I said, upset. "Seriously, there's just so much damage done, and I'm not just talking about this stupid hideout."

"What *are* you talking about?" she asked.

I glanced over my shoulder. There were other students walking closely behind us. They didn't have their robes on, but I knew they were part of my ninja clan. I made sure to speak loudly enough so they all could hear. "I'm talking about *everything*. From the first week of school, this has just been problem after problem! First Wyatt, then stealing from the food drive, and then Carlyle and that whole pirate thing, and now *this?* Someone stole my outfit and turned it into a *disaster!* They stole a note from my bag and smeared it all over the school! Why? I don't know, but I'm sure it's got *something* to do with being a ninja! Now I have to eat lunch *alone*, and Faith is *crushed!*"

Nobody responded, which made me happy.

When we arrived in front of where the hideout used to be, everyone stopped walking. It wasn't weird because other students were already there watching tractors push trees around. The whole area was already mostly cleared out, which means they must've started work on it the night before. The two hall monitors were standing at the edge of the demolition, pointing at spots in the woods and talking.

With an orange construction vest on, Gavin approached us. He was holding a short stack of papers that looked like blueprints for bleachers they were clearing the woods for. "Morning, fellas," he said.

Some of the kids acknowledged him.

I stepped forward, curious as to how much he knew. "So what'd you find in there? I think I see some rusty lockers over there," I said, pointing to the spot by the porta-potties.

Gavin nodded and pulled his aviator glasses down on his nose. "You sure do. After school yesterday, we were given a tip that a ninja was spotted around the trees here."

"Yeah?" I asked.

"Yep," Gavin replied. "Sure enough, when me and the boys investigated, we found that the problem was *worse* than the school thought."

"How so?"

The captain of the hall monitors pointed to where the ninja hideout *used* to be. "Well, there's plenty of evidence that suggests there was way *more* than just one. It was more like a whole *team* of crazy kids in ninja costumes."

"Ya don't say," I said coldly, biting my lower lip.

Gavin nodded and took a deep breath. He exhaled loudly as he spoke. "Ain't exactly sure what they were planning on doing, but it couldn't have been good, right? A whole herd of ninjas running around in the woods? *That* can't be normal."

"No," I said. "Can't be."

"Principal Davis says they've been wanting to extend the track and field out here," Gavin said. "So he was real quick to give us the go ahead to clear it out."

"What if you've got the wrong guys?" I asked, immediately regretting it.

Gavin paused and looked right at me. His eyes told me that his brain was running at full speed. Finally, he spoke. "What do ya mean – the *wrong* guys?"

"Nothing," I said before he was finished talking. "Nevermind. I just think the decision to mow down the woods was made too quickly. That's all."

Gavin chewed his lip and looked at me. It was uncomfortable because I *knew* I said too much. Please just leave it at that! Don't ask me anything else, or I might say something stupid!

Like he could read my mind, he spun on his heel and started walking away. "Ya'll have a good one now, y'hear?"

Brayden leaned closer to me and whispered. "Is Gavin the team leader for the construction crew too?"

I shrugged my shoulders and started walking the track again. "Whatever, I don't care."

"Wait!" Brayden cried. "Where are you going?"

I didn't look back. "I just want to be alone."

It was only me that walked away. Everyone else stayed to watch the crew slice up logs with their chainsaws. If it weren't my entire life for the past two months they were destroying, I probably would've thought it was cool too.

Wednesday. 11:30 AM. Lunch.

Feeling a little sick to my stomach, I decided to skip lunch. I didn't feel like sitting alone anyway. I hung out in the lobby of the school again, waiting as time slowly ticked by, hoping that nobody else would join me.

I grabbed the straps of my book bag and took a seat on the floor, leaning back against the brick wall, but it only lasted for about half a second. I saw another copy of my note taped to the lockers farther down the hallway. Sighing, I stood up and started walking away from the lobby.

Carlyle suddenly stepped out of the boy's bathroom next to cafeteria.

I stopped in place, shocked because I hadn't seen him in about a month.

He looked at me and spoke. "What're ya lookin' at, matey?'

I sighed, remembering how much I *hate* hearing kids talk like pirates. "When I figure it out, I'll let you know."

The fake pirate boy chuckled as he glanced at the copy of my note on the locker down the hall. "Seems ye have your hands full this week, eh? Fate be not in your favor."

I paused, confused. "What?"

"You've run into some pretty bad luck," Carlyle said with a smirk.

And then I decided to bluff him. "I *know* it was you and your goons! You think I'm totally stupid? You and your little pirate buddies are behind all this, and I'm about to expose you for the bully you are!"

Carlyle folded his arms and glared at me. "What evidence have ye?"

I stared back at him, but said nothing.

His eyebrows raised and he put his palms out as if he were pleading. "No really, what's the evidence ya have against me and my... *buddies?*"

"More than you know," I said, lying through my teeth. "And enough to make it so you end up at the same school as your cousin, Wyatt."

Carlyle furrowed his brow, confused. Finally, he said, "Surely you've heard..."

I had no idea what he was talking about.

He laughed heartily. "Ya haven't heard yet? Oy, matey, I'm *sorry*, but that's just *too* good!"

"What're you talking about?" I shouted at the

pirate. "What haven't I heard yet?"

Walking away, Carlyle wiped the tears from his eyes as he chuckled. "Matey, your fate be *sealed*, and ye won't even see it coming."

Clenching my fists, I watched as Carlyle walked back into the lunchroom. What in the world was the boy talking about, I wondered.

What *haven't* I heard?

Shaking my head, I continued walking toward the copy of my note. It was only yesterday that I saw the kid in red hanging one of these up, I thought. And they were actually doing it around lunchtime. I was so tired of this whole thing that I just wanted it to be over, but there was a small fire inside me that kept telling me to investigate. I might not have my ninja robes, but that didn't mean I *wasn't* a ninja at heart.

First, I tore down the copy of my note. Crumpling it in my hands, I then dropped it into one of the trashcans built into the wall.

"Where are you?" I asked softly as I walked down the hallway.

Taking the same path as the day before, I found myself in the science wing of the school again. The thief dropped his smoke bomb off here, and then disappeared into Mr. Lien's classroom. Just like before, when I peeked through the windows, the lights were off and the room was dark. I set my hand on the door handle and jiggled it, expecting it to be locked.

But it *wasn't*.

I pushed down slowly and heard it click open. And then I started pushing it open, but something else caught my eye. There was a red piece of fabric peeking out from under the door. As I studied it, I was disappointed because I realized it wasn't the same material as a sweatshirt. Instead, it looked like shiny silk.

Why would shiny silk stick out from under a classroom door?

I took a defensive stance in case it was a trap and slowly pushed the door open. "Hello?" I asked, feeling stupid. If this *wasn't* a trap then I just gave myself away.

Luckily there was no answer. Once the door was open about a foot wide, I slipped in and shut it quietly.

The inside of Mr. Lien's classroom was dark. There were no windows since it wasn't a room on the edge of the school. I waited a moment, allowing my eyes adjust. My foot slipped on the red silk on the ground. I knelt down and picked it up, holding it up to the window of the door. The light from the hallway was shining through so that helped me see exactly what it was.

I let the fabric slip through my fingers and fully unfold in front of me. There were four pieces to the cloth – pants, a long sleeved shirt, a black belt, and a mask. My jaw dropped as I realized what I was holding. It was a ninja uniform – a *red* ninja uniform.

Suddenly I heard another click from behind me and a door open. I balled up the ninja outfit and slid across the floor, behind Mr. Lien's desk.

"Can you believe this whole thing is working?" said

a boy's voice.

"Crazy, isn't it?" replied a girl. "I'd have thought Chase would've been smarter than he is, but as it turns out, he's just as dumb as everyone else."

"They're out there destroying the old hideout. Won't be long now until he's completely powerless and without a ninja clan of his own."

The girl laughed. "Then the red ninja clan will *rise* and take control of this school."

The red ninja clan? The kid who took my bag *was* wearing a red hoodie. Could he have something to do with them?

"We better get out of here quick, or we won't have time to eat lunch," said the boy.

"Mm-hmm. Training can take a lot out of a kid, right?"

I heard the door to the room click open and then shut again. Peeking my head over Mr. Lien's desk, I scanned the dark for anyone else. There was nobody.

As silently as possible, I started walking along the edge of the room. The two kids had come from somewhere, right? Two kids don't just appear out of nowhere. Besides, I heard the first door they walked out of.

The farther into the room I walked, the darker is was. I ran my fingers along the wall, feeling for a door and then… I found it. It was a door at the back of the room, but I had no idea where it led.

And then I heard a familiar sound, like people were jumping around on the other side of the door. Pressing my ear against the wood confirmed that they *were* people in the next room. *Many* people.

I pulled the door open just a crack, enough so that I could see through the slit. In the secret room next to the one I was in, I saw several kids wearing ninja robes. *Red* ninja robes. They were different from the robes my clan wore – the red ninjas had armor plating on their shoulders and chest. I have to admit it looked cool.

I couldn't be sure of how many ninjas there were because the crowd was so large that I lost count. From where I was standing, I wasn't able to tell who the leader was either. He was probably somewhere near the front of the ninja clan, overseeing their training.

I let the door shut slowly as I headed to the exit of the classroom. I was lucky enough that I wasn't seen by any of the red ninjas, but if I watched any longer, *someone* would see me.

Back in the hallway of the school, I let Mr. Lien's classroom door shut and walked back to the lobby of the school. The other kids were still eating lunch, and I had a few minutes until fifth period science class. That was enough time to try and wrap my head around I had witnessed.

A group of students had formed another ninja clan at Buchanan, that part was obvious. They had to be the ones behind all the garbage that happened this week. I bet *they* were the ones who stole my note to Faith *and* my ninja outfit! *They* were the ones who got that *photo* taken in my black ninja robes! *They* were the ones that tipped Gavin off to the ninja hideout that led to its destruction!

"Chase?" a girl's voice suddenly asked, catching me off guard.

"Huh?" I grunted, turning around.

Faith was standing outside the cafeteria with Zoe by her side. I didn't know what to say so I smiled at her.

"Hi," Faith said, folding her arms.

"Hey," I replied. Not wanting to miss the opportunity, I quickly spoke again. "Look, I'm sorry about yesterday. Really, I am. I'm sorry about this whole thing. If I could take it back, I would."

"I know," Faith said softly.

"I told her everything," Zoe added.

When I made eye contact with Zoe, I knew what she meant. She told Faith I was a ninja.

I stepped forward. "But that *wasn't* me in the school paper!"

Faith nodded. "I know that too. Zoe told me you were framed. And then she told me about Wyatt and the food drive at the beginning of the year plus Carlyle and the pirate invasion last month."

I scratched the back of my head, embarrassed. "Yeah, that was all me too."

She grinned. "That was pretty cool of you."

"Yeah?"

She paused. "Yeah."

"Bell's about to ring," Zoe said as she started walking down the hallway.

Faith jogged to catch up with her as students from the cafeteria started filling the lobby.

Before they got too far, I spoke again. "So does this mean you don't hate me?"

Faith spun around with a smile on her face, but didn't answer. She didn't have to. I knew what she meant.

So to recap my Wednesday – my own ninja hideout had been destroyed *permanently*, I found out there's a *red ninja clan* training in a secret room of the school, I saw *Carlyle* for the first time in a month, he also hinted at something *terrible* in my future, Gavin was *clearly* on a mission to expose the ninja clan that he doesn't know is *my* ninja clan, the copies of my note were still lingering around Buchanan...

But Faith didn't *hate* me.

All in all, this *wasn't* the worst day ever.

Thursday. 7:45 AM. Homeroom.

Though it seemed like Faith was cool with me, it was still embarrassing for us to sit together in science. I'm not surprised at all though since the teasing hadn't completely stopped.

It was enough for me though. The rest of the day went smoother than the whole week had. Even Zoe noticed it in homeroom.

"You seem chipper today," she said, taking her usual spot at the desk in front of me.

"Meh," I replied, shrugging my shoulders.

"Any reason why?" she asked.

"I just feel like it's going to be a good day," I said.

"Me too," Brayden added as he entered the room. "I think your luck is about to completely turn around today."

That was odd of Brayden to suggest such a thing,

but I went with it. "You think so?" I asked.

"Yeah," he said, nodding. "In fact, I *know* it."

Zoe turned toward him. "How can you know something like that?"

"I don't know," he answered. "I can just feel it… in the *air*. Know what I mean?"

Zoe and I laughed. Mrs. Robinson started with the morning announcements.

"Again, if you plan on eating pizza tomorrow night at the skate party, bring two dollars extra. The school is fronting the money for admission so if anyone needs a ride, there will be a couple busses leaving here at 4:45 so *obviously* don't miss those. Be here around 4:30 or so."

Zoe turned in her chair. "My dad will pick you up tomorrow. Don't forget."

"What if I don't want to go?" I asked, feeling nervous that the teasing probably wasn't over. If kids were this mean *at* school, just imagine what they'd say *outside* of school!

"You don't have a choice," my cousin said. "If you're worried about people making fun of you, then the best thing you can do is to stand tall and let them know you don't care about what anyone says about you."

"But I *do* care," I whispered.

"I *know* you do," she said, bluntly, "which is why you should go tomorrow night."

There was no use arguing with Zoe. She was just like her mom, who was also my aunt. "Alright, I'll go," I said. To be honest, there was a small part of me that was happy about the decision, but don't get me wrong – I still wasn't looking forward to it.

Thursday. 8:25 AM. Art class.

I was the last one in the room before the bell rang. Zoe and Brayden were in the middle of a conversation as I dropped my book bag next to my seat.

"But who could've tipped them off?" Zoe asked quietly.

Brayden shrugged his shoulders. "I don't know. Didn't you see it? There were like, tractors and chainsaws and stuff. Gavin was running around like he owned the place."

"No," Zoe said. "I was in the gym playing volleyball. I *knew* I should've walked the track."

I joined the conversation. "Yeah, the whole hideout is gone."

"Everything?" Zoe asked, shocked.

"All of it," I said. "It's not like there was much to begin with, but it doesn't matter because it's been

69

completely flattened out."

"Do you know who told Gavin?" Zoe asked.

"No," I said, "but I *might* have a clue."

Brayden sat up straight. "What? You mean you know who exposed the hideout?"

I shook my head. "Not exactly *who*, but I think I know what *group* might have."

"A group?" Zoe asked. "Oh great, not another pirate takeover I hope."

"No, it's much worse," I said, leaning closer to my cousin and friend. "Yesterday, I was investigating a lead I had…"

"A lead?" Zoe said. "Are you some kind of detective now?"

I ignored her comment and continued. "The other day I saw the kid in red and chased after him."

Brayden chuckled. "Uh, yeah. That happened on Monday. Everyone knows that."

"No, I saw that kid again on Tuesday! I chased after him, but lost him when he disappeared into a classroom."

Zoe pouted. "Go on…"

"So yesterday, I checked out the classroom when no one was there," I said. "I found out there's another ninja clan at this school, a *red* ninja clan."

Brayden gasped. "No way," he whispered.

"Of *course* there is," Zoe sighed. "Buchanan can't just be a *normal* school with *normal* kids who *don't* form secret societies of ninjas or plan crazy pirate takeovers… I wonder if there's still time to open enroll at another school."

"What should we do?" Brayden asked, seriously concerned.

"I don't know," I answered, tapping my fingers on the desk. "I haven't thought that far ahead yet."

"What about your speech yesterday?" Brayden said. "The one you made in gym class?"

"What speech?" Zoe asked.

Brayden answered too quickly for me to say anything. "He basically said he was done with everything." And then he looked back at me. "Are you saying there's still a chance at having a ninja clan at this school? I mean, not the red ninja clan, but *your* ninja clan?"

"I'm willing to bet that if you just did nothing," Zoe said, "then this whole thing would just blow over."

"I'm thinking that too," I said.

"But you *can't* do *nothing!*" Brayden whispered. "Now that you know something bad is going down, you *have* to do something! Don't you have a *responsibility* to? What's that famous saying? With great responsibility comes great power? Is that right? Yeah, that's right. I think the first astronaut said it or something."

Zoe's jaw dropped. "*Wow*, you are *so* wrong about that quote, it's not even funny. It's *sad.* You're a *sad* little boy."

I shrugged my shoulders and looked at Brayden. "Zoe might be right. Maybe the best thing to do… is nothing."

Brayden folded his arms and sunk in his chair. "Fine then. *Don't* do anything about it. I guess we'll just see what happens when the red ninja clan takes over the whole school."

I felt a chill run down my spine, but did my best to ignore it. For some reason Brayden was really upset about this, but I thought that with time, he'd come to appreciate the decision to leave it all alone. Maybe not today. Maybe not in high school. But someday in the future…

Yeah. He'll *totally* do that.

*Thursday. 11:25 AM. Right after gym class
and right before lunch.*

I walked the track in gym again, but this time I
actually *walked* the track. The demolition crew was still
there, but at this point in the week, they were mostly just
cleaning up after themselves. The wooded area that we
used for our ninja training was surprisingly smaller than I
thought so I was a bit taken back at how quickly it
disappeared.

Zoe walked with Brayden and I. She hadn't seen
what all the hype was about, but wanted to. The rest of
gym was spent making boring small talk about the
weather or things like that.

But now I was waiting for lunch to start in the
lobby of the school. Students with a high GPA were
allowed to take their lunch into the library if they wanted
to do some extra studying or research something on the

73

computer. That's where Zoe was at the moment.

Brayden was supposed to be around. It was possible he was in the lobby somewhere, but because there were so many other kids waiting to enter the cafeteria, I didn't see him.

As soon as the bell rang, students crammed through the doors of the lunchroom, forming a line so they could get their food. From the smell of it, I think they were serving taco pizza.

I waited at the back of the crowd until they were all through the door. Then I took a seat on one of the benches in the lobby. Eating alone wasn't awful – at least today I brought a sandwich.

Reaching into my bag, I grabbed the brown paper sack I packed this morning, but before I could pull it out, I heard a bunch of shouting come from down the hall.

"Don't let him get away!" shouted a boy.

"Cut him off, sir!"

"Freeze right there, mister! Ain't no way you're gettin' away this time!"

About fifty feet away, I saw someone turn the corner and start tearing through the hallway toward me. Behind them was Gavin along with his two hall monitors. They were in hot pursuit of someone that looked like a shadow.

Their footsteps grew louder as they all sprinted as fast as they could. I felt my heart start racing when I saw what it was that the hall monitors were chasing after. It was a ninja, but not one of the red ones – the ninja was wearing *black*. And I bet it was *my* black uniform they had.

As the ninja approached, he didn't swerve or anything. I guess he thought he was just gonna plow through the lobby unnoticed?

Gavin and his hall monitors were still a ways back so I jumped forward, hoping to catch the kid that'd been making my life so miserable this week.

But all of a sudden, *somebody else* jumped in front of me. They moved so quickly that all I saw was a red blur. I heard a loud thump as I watched the ninja get tackled to the ground by...

The kid in the red hooded sweatshirt!

My mind went nuts trying to understand what it was that I was seeing. The kid in red was supposed to be the one in my ninja uniform running from Gavin, but instead, I was watching the kid in red wrestle with... *who?*

I kept my distance as Gavin and his hall monitors approached. The mysterious kid's red hood was up and over his face, just as it always had been, so I couldn't see who it was. Just the other day I saw him putting up a copy of one of my notes! I *knew* he was guilty and the one who stole my book bag so *who was he chasing?*

"Thanks," Gavin said, catching his breath.

The kid in the red hoodie stood and dusted himself off. The hall monitors grabbed the ninjas arms and brought him to his feet.

"Not a problem," said the boy in red.

Gavin paused, taking a step backward when he

looked at the face under the red shroud. "You..."

Most of the kids from the cafeteria had their faces pressed up against the tinted glass walls, absorbed by what was taking place in the lobby. A few of them even left their place in line to come out.

The kid in red lifted his hand up, waved to the other students and turned slowly. *Who was under the red hood? It was killing me that he wasn't turning around so I could see!*

And then finally, the boy in red grabbed the sides of his hood and flipped it backward. He turned around and looked at me with the coldest eyes I'd ever seen.

It was *Wyatt*.

WYATT!

WHAAAT??

If you heard a small pop, don't worry. It was just

my brain exploding.

"Hello!" Wyatt sneered.

Several of the kids watching gasped loudly. It was like one of those moments from a movie where everyone is shocked at the same time.

I couldn't speak, mostly because I couldn't breath. Last month, Carlyle *said* Wyatt was going to return, but I didn't think it was possible. How is it that someone can come back to a school they were *expelled* from?

Wyatt spun in place and ripped the black mask off the ninja. I felt my knees suddenly grow weak. The ninja Gavin was chasing after was my best friend – it was Brayden.

"Looks like we've caught our thief," Wyatt said, bluntly.

"It wasn't me!" Brayden shouted as the two hall monitors kept him in place.

Gavin didn't move. "What're you doin' back at this school?"

"Am I not welcome here?" Wyatt asked.

Another voice came from the crowd. "Of course you are!" said a short boy wearing a gray suit as he stepped forward. It was Buchanan School's president. "Wyatt is a friend and student here at Buchanan."

Gavin stood at attention. "But sir," he said, "Wyatt was *expelled* from Buchanan at the end of the first week."

The president wagged his finger back and forth. "That's not true. He was *never* expelled, but merely *suspended* for a short period of time."

"Suspended?" Gavin asked. "But everyone said he'd been *expelled*."

"Nobody actually said anything," the president replied. "Teachers won't comment on a thing like that and when they don't deny or confirm anything, everyone assumes the worst. It's a backwards system, I know. Nobody's allowed to say anything so that it doesn't *spread gossip*, but the lack of saying anything is actually what *creates gossip*."

I decided to speak up. "But it's been *two months!* Nobody gets suspended for *two months!*"

Wyatt nodded. "Yes, it has been *awhile*, hasn't it?"

"Explain yourself!" I shouted.

Wyatt lifted his hands as if he were surrendering. "Easy now. I was suspended for the maximum time – two weeks. After that, my parents decided to see how I'd do if I were home schooled... needless to say I drove them *crazy*."

The crowd laughed at Wyatt's joke.

Gavin folded his arms and planted his feet.

The president put his arm around Wyatt and spoke to the crowd. "Wyatt did a good thing today! He rescued the school from the petty ninja! I think that's enough to redeem the boy in everyone's eyes, isn't it?"

I wanted to tell everyone about how Wyatt stole my book bag at the beginning of the week. About how he photocopied my note and hung it up all over. About how he wore my ninja outfit and caused chaos... but I didn't say it. I didn't need any more attention than I'd already gotten.

I looked at Brayden, but said nothing.

"I just wanted to help," Brayden said, staring at the ground so it wasn't obvious he was speaking to me. "It wasn't *me* pictured in the school paper. I know there's more going on in secret, and I just wanted to uncover it for the whole school to see."

"How very *noble* of you," Wyatt said sarcastically.

"If I solved this case," Brayden continued, "then the school would know the truth – that it's not the black ninja clan that's the problem."

"Take him away, boys," said the president.

The two monitors pulled Brayden away. Gavin hesitated, staring daggers at Wyatt, but finally turned and joined the other two hall monitors.

"Shows over, guys," the president said. "You can all go back to your lunch now."

I watched as Brayden was taken into the principal's office. I think I felt the ground shake as the door slammed shut.

Everyone else filtered through the cafeteria doors. Wyatt brushed his hand down his red hooded sweatshirt and glanced at me. With a smirk, he headed my way. This was the kid that beat the tar out of me in the first week of school. He was the kid that stole money from the student food drive and tried to frame my cousin for it. And now he was the kid that stole my backpack and killed my social life.

I realized at that moment… I was afraid of him.

Wyatt extended his hand toward me. "Sorry about all that stuff the first week of school."

I stared at the back of his hand and remembered how he used it to hit me. Then I looked into his eyes. "You won't get away with all this."

His eyes narrowed as his smirk grew wider. "I think we already have," he said.

"We?" I asked.

"You didn't think Carlyle was *done* with you, did you?" Wyatt asked.

I said nothing.

"Together," Wyatt continued with his hand still presented to me, "we'll make sure your defeat is final, but not before a little bit of *punishment* first." And then he nodded at the window of students still watching us. "If I were you, I'd shake hands with me. You don't want to look like the smaller man here, do you?"

I paused, thinking on it. It was as if he were challenging me, and if all I had to do was take his hand and accept the challenge, then so be it. I clutched at his hand and squeezed.

He shook once and let go. Stepping through the cafeteria doors, he didn't look back.

I could feel my face getting hot as I clenched my fists, but I felt a pinch in the hand that was just touching Wyatt's. When I opened it, a folded piece of paper fell to the floor. Using my foot, I smeared it sideways, pushing it open so I could see what it was.

I sighed, realizing it was the original copy of my note to Faith. I already knew Wyatt was behind this week's terrible events, and he *knew* that *I* knew, but what he wanted to show me… was that he didn't care.

Friday. 7:45 AM. Homeroom.

"So you just *let* Gavin take him away?" was the first thing Zoe said when she walked in the door to homeroom.

I knew she was talking about Brayden. "What could I do? He got himself caught!"

"You could've at least said *something!*"

"Brayden knew what he was doing."

Zoe shook her head. "I thought you two were best friends? It even sounds like he was the one trying to help *you!*"

I sat forward in my desk. "I told him I wasn't going to do anything about this. I said it wasn't worth fighting over because any action I took would just make it worse!"

"Funny," Zoe said. "Even your inaction has caused trouble."

"No," I said. "*Wyatt* caused trouble."

Zoe nodded. "I heard about that. That's all anyone talked about yesterday. He saved the school from the dreaded ninja... who happened to be Brayden."

"I don't want to say that Wyatt is an evil genius," I said, "but it sure seems to look that way."

"He's just lucky," Zoe replied. "The story kids are telling has Wyatt wearing a red hooded sweatshirt. They call him the 'Red Shrouded Hero.'"

"*Hero?*" I whispered, angry.

Zoe leaned closer. "He caught the ninja everyone was after! You know how people can flip their opinions of someone in a heartbeat! It's almost like kids *wanted* him to be good! Who *doesn't* love a redemption story?"

I took a deep breath. "I don't know what to do about this whole thing. I'm not really in the mood to get punched in the face again. I'm far too pretty for that."

Zoe paused, snickering. Then she changed the subject. "Skate party's still happening tonight whether you want it to or not, you know."

"Figured that," I said. "I'll have to get through the day first. TGIF, right?"

Zoe stared at me. Finally, she asked, "What's TGIF mean?"

I shrugged my shoulders. "I dunno. I thought *you'd* know."

"Weirdo," she said, smiling.

With Brayden possibly in detention and the rest of my ninjas keeping a low profile, I had nobody else I could count on for help, except for Zoe. The threat of the red ninja clan was real, but she'd never believe me unless she saw it with her own eyes. "Do me a favor?"

She raised her eyebrows.

"Meet me in the lobby before the end of lunch," I said. "Around 11:45 or so."

"Why?" she asked. "Are you planning something terrible?"

I shook my head and laughed. "No, nothing like that. I just… I need your help. There's something I need to show you."

Zoe took a breath. "I don't think anything good has ever come after that sentence is uttered."

"Just trust me," I said.

Friday. Around 11:45 AM.
Toward the end of lunch.

The rest of the morning was uneventful, which to me was a good thing. Boring was safe. I was alone again in the lobby, having eaten my entire sandwich on the bench outside the cafeteria. I kept staring at the spot where Wyatt tackled Brayden. I'm not sure why.

"So I'm here," Zoe said.

I jumped, bumping my head against the brick wall.

"Easy, tiger," she said.

Rubbing the back of my head, I spoke. "You scared me. I must've zoned out."

"Right," she said, glancing over her shoulder. "So what is it you wanted to show me?"

I got up and started walking away from the cafeteria and down the hall. As she followed, I continued talking. "The other day I caught Wyatt hanging up a copy of my

85

note, except at the time I didn't *know* it was Wyatt."

Zoe wasn't surprised. "I know. You told us in art."

"I chased after him down this hallway," I said, pointing farther down the corridor. "But when he rounded the corner, he disappeared." I stepped around the corner and approached Mr. Lien's classroom door. "He disappeared into *this* room."

Zoe stepped forward and grabbed the handle of the door. She pushed it down and once again, it wasn't locked. "Did you go in? What happened?"

"The first time I went in, I didn't see anything," I explained. "Wyatt just disappeared. But I went back the next day to investigate it some more."

"Course you did," Zoe sighed.

Opening the door, I stepped into the room and put my finger to my lips, telling Zoe we had to be quiet. As we walked to the door in the back of the room, I whispered. "I found this other door and when I opened it... I saw what Wyatt has been busy doing."

Zoe was confused. "Was he working on a science fair project or something?"

"Ew, no," I replied. "He's been busy building another ninja clan. Remember? I told you I saw a *red* ninja clan."

Zoe continued to sneak through the room with me. I couldn't see her face, but her voice told me she was rolling her eyes. "I'd say you were full of bologna, and that you're just talking crazy now, but then I remembered there was a secret ninja clan that used to train in the woods... so I'll take your word for it."

I put my finger to my lips again, and stared at her until she nodded. Then I placed my hand on the handle of the red ninja's secret entrance and pushed it down as quietly as possible. There was barely a click, but it sounded like a gun went off. I held my breath and waited a moment. When nothing happened, I pushed the door open half an inch.

Zoe stepped up to the slit in the door and stared through it. After a second, she spoke. "What am I looking at?"

"Ninjas! There are ninjas training in there!" I whispered.

"No," she said, standing up. "There's nobody in

that room."

Pushing her out of the way, I pressed my face against the open space. She was right. There weren't any red ninjas in the next room. "That's impossible. Where could they be?"

"Here!" a shrill voice shouted as the fluorescent lights flickered on overhead.

The sudden light was blinding as I spun around. Pain shot through my head and down my spine as I covered my eyes. *"Zoe, what's happening?"*

"I think we've found your red ninjas," I heard her say.

When I opened my eyes, I saw three members of the red ninja clan, standing near the entrance of Mr. Lien's classroom. They were dressed in their red silk robes and closing in on us.

"You'll pay for your actions," said one of the red ninjas at the front. "Our leader, Wyatt, has told us to send you a message. You're *done* at Buchanan."

Grabbing Zoe's arm, I flung the door wide open and pushed her through. Hopefully Zoe was right and there weren't any other red ninjas training in there. "Go!" I shouted.

Instantly, Zoe started running through the dark room. I jumped through the door, pulling it shut. Sliding my hand across the surface of the door, I couldn't find a lock. There wasn't any time to keep searching so I started backing away. One of the red ninjas twisted the handle and started pushing it open. I threw my body forward, slamming it shut again. I could hear the other ninjas colliding with the closed door.

"Come on!" cried Zoe.

Buchanan School has this weird feature where every room has an entrance at the front, but also a door on the wall that goes into the next classroom, completely bypassing the hallway. I think they built it like that in case of emergencies. If there were ever a fire in the hallway, students and faculty could use these other doors to leave the building.

I did my best to avoid the desks, but the new room was so dark that it was hard to see. Instead of a swift getaway, I tumbled across the floor.

The red ninjas poured into the dark room and continued chasing after me. I didn't know what they were planning on doing, but I sure didn't want to find out.

Crawling across the carpet, I grabbed a desk leg and pulled myself up. Spinning around to see how close the ninjas were, I saw a foot come at my face. I dodged it, rolling backwards across the desk, and landing perfectly on my feet. A bit of excitement sent a chill through my body, and I couldn't help but smile.

"I'll rip that smile from your face!" cried another red ninja as he dove at me.

This time, I hopped off one of the chairs and jumped across the room, over to where Zoe was holding another door open.

"Quickly!" she shouted waving me into the next room.

I grabbed the door and gestured for Zoe to walk through. "Ladies first!"

Suddenly, I was pushed to the floor, but tumbled until I was back on my feet. The other ninjas jumped through the door one by one. And then one of them started running toward Zoe.

"Chase!" she cried.

As they reached their hands out for her, I pushed against a chair with my foot, sliding it across the floor. The red ninja stumbled, tripping over the chair and fell to the ground.

Clutching Zoe's hand, I started running for the front entrance of the classroom. There was no way these red ninjas would risk going into the hallway, would they?

I opened the door and glanced over my shoulder. The red ninja that I tripped was trying to stand up, but the other two were still coming after us. I guess they meant business.

Zoe and I started running down the hall, back toward the cafeteria. It felt like a bad dream. No matter how fast we ran, it didn't feel fast enough. I kept looking back to see if the red ninjas had left the room yet.

Suddenly, I felt a strong hand grab my arm. It yanked me into another dark classroom. My hand was still gripping my cousin's so she fell right in there with me. Then I heard the click of a door locking.

"Keep your heads down," said a boy's voice. "Hopefully they'll pass by, and we'll be alright."

Through the window of the door, I saw a line of red blurs pass in front of it. The red ninjas *had* chased us into the hallway but had no idea where we had gone.

Ha! Take *that* red ninjas!

After my eyes adjusted to the dark again, I looked at the kid who saved us. It was Gavin, the captain of the hall monitors. "But why'd you help us?"

Gavin stared through the tiny window of the door. "That whole thing that went down yesterday with your friend Brayden? Somethin' was fishy about it. The way the president was so keen on lettin' Wyatt off the hook for his crimes just felt... *off.*"

"What're you saying?" Zoe asked, catching her breath.

"I ain't sayin' anything specific now," Gavin replied. "Just sayin' somethin's *off* about it."

The bell rang, signaling the end of the lunch. The students rushing through the hallway was a welcome sound. The red ninjas chased us in an empty hallway, but I knew they wouldn't stick around when it was full of children. No ninja was *that* stupid.

"Brayden's innocent," I whispered.

Gavin nodded. "I suspected that. He just moves too goofy to be a real ninja. Clumsy and all that. Plus when Principal Davis was questioning him, he had all sorts of stuff to say about Wyatt and his involvement with the ninja clan."

I felt my cheek twitch. "Really? What'd he say?"

"He kept sayin' it was Wyatt and Carlyle who were up to the nonsense this week that involved your little love note and the photo of the ninja in the school paper," Gavin sighed.

"I don't know about Carlyle," I said, "but it was Wyatt for sure."

"Brayden mentioned Wyatt stole your backpack on Monday," Gavin said. "Is that right?"

"Mm hmm," I hummed. "And I also saw him hanging up a copy of my note."

Gavin paused, looking out the small window of the door. "You're one of them, aren't ya?"

I remained silent, but Zoe put her hands on to her mouth and squawked. Thanks, Zoe, for totally giving me away.

"You wouldn't be gettin' chased after unless they had a reason," Gavin explained. "And those other kids were dressed in red ninja costumes. The one *I'm* after wears a black costume. Normally when I see a *group* of kids chasing *one* kid with a girl by his side... I'd bet my money that it's the *one* kid that's innocent."

I didn't know what to say, but a bunch of sounds mumbled out of my mouth anyway. "But I... um... it's kinda... well..."

Gavin laughed. "Your secret's safe with me. Is that what you want to hear?"

"It is," I said.

Gavin swung the door open and nodded his head at Zoe. "Ladies first."

"Thank you!" Zoe said, blushing as she stepped through the door, glancing back at me. "Sounds better when *he* says it."

As Zoe and I stepped into the hallway, Gavin

spoke. "I got a little pull with Principal Davis. I'll let him know what I think about Brayden, and hopefully he'll listen."

"Where's Brayden *been* today?" Zoe asked.

"He got 'all-day-detention'," Gavin replied.

I shuddered. "Ouch."

Gavin joined the other students as they walked through the hall. Zoe and I split up to swap our books out at our lockers. With Wyatt and the threat of the red ninjas looming over me, it felt good to have someone new on our side – someone with some official authority at Buchanan. I wasn't sure what Gavin was capable of, but I was just happy he was one of the good guys.

I was sure I'd still hear some shouts about my love note. For the most part, the teasing died down. Of course there would always be stragglers, but that's what you get when you're around kids your own age. It didn't matter. Faith was in my next class, and we were still lab partners. That was enough for me.

There was still half a day left and a few classes to trudge through before the weekend officially started… oh yeah, *and* a skate party I had to attend.

Friday. 5:00 PM.
Right before the skating party.

I stepped out of the car that Zoe's dad drove. We had just arrived, and my rollerblades were slung over my shoulder. Already running to the entrance of the skating rink was my younger sister, more excited than I'd ever seen in my life. Third graders had no idea how *easy* they had it.

"Thanks, dad!" Zoe said, shutting the door.

Her father rolled the window down. "I'll be here at seven, alright? You have your phone on you?"

Zoe pulled her cell phone out of her pocket. Then she rolled her eyes and groaned. "Yesssss, it's right here, dad."

"You got your two bucks for pizza?" her dad asked.

"Yesssss!" she answered, loudly.

Her dad, my uncle, pointed at me. "What about you,

pal? You got two bucks?"

I nodded with my hands in my pockets.

"See ya, dad!" Zoe said, letting him know he could leave at anytime.

"Love you!" he shouted from the car.

I flinched, feeling pain for Zoe. A parent shouting, *"I love you,"* from a car was the *worst* thing they could do to their child! Didn't her dad *know* this? Didn't he get the *memo?*

She smiled. "Love you too!"

I looked around at the other kids who were being dropped off, waiting for someone to tease her, but nobody did. Huh… guess I was wrong about that.

"Wait up!" I yelled as I jogged to Zoe's side. My stomach started to gurgle. "I'm having second thoughts about this."

"It's fine," Zoe said with a hop in her step. "It'll be fun, really. And who cares? If anyone says anything, just ignore them!"

"Easier said than done," I replied.

"I know," Zoe said. "But the best thing you can do is let it slip right past you. Anyone who says anything is just being a turd. If you lash out at them or try fighting back, it just makes things worse."

"Maybe."

"Tell me," she said. "What do you think would happen if you freaked out?"

I thought about it for a moment and then answered. "I don't know."

"They'd get the response they were looking for," Zoe explained. "Kids who tease are doing it to make someone else feel bad, whether they know it or not. If you can show them you don't give a spew about it, then I'd be surprised if they kept doing it."

I hated when Zoe had a point. "Right."

"Don't just say 'right,'" she said. "How old are you?"

"Eleven," I replied.

"Eleven years old is almost an adult! You'll be shaving soon!" she joked. "You're really gonna let a couple of kids tease you about liking a girl who *might* actually like you back?"

I stopped walking, floored. "What? Did Faith say something about me?"

Zoe fumbled over her words as she started walking faster. "What? *Nothing!* Nevermind! I didn't say anything!"

Smiling, I let her walk ahead of me until she disappeared through the doors of the skating rink. Breathing deeply, I felt the cool air fill my lungs. Maybe this whole thing wouldn't be as difficult as I feared it was going to be.

Boy, was I ever wrong...

Friday. 5:10 PM. The skating party.

I walked to the table where Zoe was already sitting. Emily and a couple of other girls were there too. There were several paper cups filled with soda on the table, along with some chewy fruit candy.

The skating rink was dark with lights that flashed on and off with the beat of the music. The bass was, as usual, over the top. I'm sure I'd recognize the song they were playing if it didn't only sound like, "BOOM, BOOM, BOOM!"

"Hey, Chase!" Emily said cheerfully. "Have a seat!"

Emily was always super nice. Even if I were a *monster*, she'd still offer me a seat. "Thanks" I said, dropping my rollerblades on the floor. I pushed my shoes off and forced my feet into my skates.

Zoe had to shout so I could hear her voice. She

pointed at my rollerblades. "So you know how to use
those things or what?"

I smiled as I pulled my laces tighter around my
ankle. "I know my way around these things, yeah!"

Pushing herself away, she rolled backward. "Race
ya!"

I watched as she skated away and onto the skating
floor. I frantically tied knots around my skates and stood.
There's always that awkward moment when you first
stand on skates – like your body has to remember how to
use them. I imagine I looked like an old man trying to
figure out what was happening with my feet. Zoe was

definitely going to win this race, but I'm pretty sure she wasn't serious anyhow.

"Sup, lover boy!" cried a voice from nearby.

I smiled at the kid who threw the insult, hoping that was the last I'd have to hear of it that night.

When I got to the skating floor, it was so packed that I had to wait until a spot opened up so I could jump in. The sixth grade class of Buchanan wasn't large by any means, but this wasn't just a sixth grader event. This was everyone from second grade up.

Finally, an empty spot opened, and I jumped forward. Gliding along, I kept the same pace as everyone else. The colorful lights spun large circles around the entire floor while they also blinked on and off. The music was even louder in the middle of the rink.

"C'mon, *Chase!*" Zoe said as she zipped past me. "You're already a lap behind! What're you gonna tell your parents when your cousin mops the floor with you?"

"That she cheated!" I replied, pushing my feet forward and gaining speed.

"*Cheated?*" Zoe asked as she spun around. She skated backwards, taunting me. "Don't be a sore loser. You don't wear that quality well."

I laughed, balling my fists up and swinging them out while I started running on my rollerblades. Weaving between slower skaters, I glanced over at Zoe. "How can I be a sore loser when I win all the time?"

As we raced each other around the skating rink, the songs switched, and the lights continued blinking. After about twenty minutes, my legs fully remembered how to maneuver on rollerblades, and I moved like my own body had grown them.

Exhausted, I rolled up to the spot on the wall where kids could exit. All that skating and racing with Zoe had me work up a sweat, and I felt like I was going to die if I didn't get something to drink immediately. Ice-cold soda was my first choice of thirst quencher.

At the concession counter, I rolled up and waited in line. There were six or seven people in front of me. The menu was filled with all kinds of junk food my parents would try to keep me away from – popcorn with too much butter, all kinds of candy bars, wrinkly hot dogs, nachos, soft pretzels, and of course… cotton candy.

I heard the girl in front of me giggle. I wasn't sure about what, but I assumed it was about me. The boy in front of her leaned out to get a good look at me.

"Hey, man," said the boy. He was taller and lankier than I was. "How'd the wedding go?"

The girl burst out laughing, covering her mouth immediately. The other kids in line turned around to see what was so funny.

I curled my lip, smiling. I wasn't sure what to say. "Good one," I muttered.

Another boy at the front of the line spoke, as if it were his turn to toss an insult. "Did you ever get a response from her? Did she hire you for the position of boyfriend yet?"

My face felt warm. "Funny," I said through my teeth. What was Zoe's suggestion? Brush it off? Ignore it? Fine, we'll try it her way.

Pointing toward the dining area, the girl in front of me spoke. "Hey, there's Faith!"

I spun in place, looking for Faith, but I couldn't see her. And then I heard everyone in the line laugh at me. I didn't turn back around, but instead skated away. Soda wasn't necessary to drink – I'm sure I could find a water fountain nearby.

I wasn't sure how much more teasing I could take. It just felt weird to have all that attention on me. Even if it was the good kind of attention, it'd still be weird, but it was the bad kind – the kind where people are laughing *at* you. Like everyone is in on the same joke, but the joke is *you.*

Finally, in a dark and scary corner of the skating rink, I found the water fountain, hidden among metal lockers. There were two of them, but the taller one didn't have a spout. The shorter fountain was rusted and smelled like metal, and when I pushed the button for water, it barely shot into the air. The extra special part about this fountain was that the water was a nice cloudy brown color. I don't know about you, but I love my water looking like gravy. Ugh… I was going to have to touch this thing with my *lips.*

Sick! It even *tasted* like gravy.

But whatever – I was away from those other kids, and I was the bigger man. I took Zoe's advice and did my best to ignore them, even skating away so they couldn't say anything anymore. This whole ignoring thing might have something to it.

Then the overhead speakers cackled.

"This next song is dedicated to two very special students at Buchanan School."

My jaw dropped as I stared at the metal speaker on the ceiling.

"*Faith, this next song is for you from your very special someone...*"

O...

"*Chase Cooper wants you to know you'll live in his heart forever...*"

M...

"*No matter how old and gross the two of you get!*"

G...

A slow jazz love song started playing. Obviously, someone else requested it, thinking it was funny.

That was it. I was stuck in the corner of the skating rink. There was no way I was going to show my face now. I had water, and if I set up some traps, I could probably catch a few mice for food. I could live happily back there.

Tales would be told of the creepy old dude who set up camp in the corner of the building. Parents would tell their children to behave or the skating rink man would find them and force them to drink gravy water from the fountain!

"Chase?" Zoe's voice said.

I didn't answer.

She rolled out from behind the lockers and pointed at one of the metal speakers on the ceiling where the music was coming from. "That'll be hard to ignore."

"Who requested that song?" I whispered, listening to the music.

Zoe paused, folding her arms. "I saw Wyatt and Carlyle skating away from the DJ right before that announcement.

Something in me snapped. I skated past Zoe and flew out into the dining area of the skating rink. A few kids thought it would be funny to applaud me as I appeared.

Scanning the room, I saw Wyatt and Carlyle off to the side, playing a game of air hockey. Pushing forward, I started moving toward them.

"Wait!" Zoe shouted from behind me.

I didn't stop, but she was able to catch up.

"What're you doing?" she asked, stopping in front of me.

"I don't know," I said. "But I think I'll figure it out when I get there."

"You're gonna start a fight, aren't you?" she asked, mad. "You know that's what they want, right?"

I didn't answer, glaring across the room at my enemies.

"Nothing would make the two of them happier than if you went over there throwing punches," Zoe said.

"What am I supposed to do?" I yelled. "Just ignore it?"

"I know it's tough, but yeah," Zoe said. "You could tell one of the teachers here."

I shook my head as I pushed her aside. "No. I'm not gonna *tell* on them. That's just gonna make it *worse*."

Zoe slid by and stopped in front of me again. "Then at least think about this before you do it!"

I sighed. "Fine, what do you mean?"

"If you go over there and start a fight," Zoe said, "then *you're* the one who started it. Sure you might get a little sympathy 'cause those two took it a *little* far, but it's still *you* who threw the first punch."

I stared at Zoe, waiting for her suggestion.

"And you know that those two want nothing else than a reason to punch back," Zoe said.

"Probably," I replied.

"So do something *different*," Zoe said. "Make them play a *different* game."

Zoe finally caught my curiosity. "Like… a 'dance off' or something?"

"You dork," Zoe said, grinning. "No, but something else like that. Teasing and picking on you is their game, so what *you* need to do is *change* the *game*."

My cousin had her moments of brilliance; I'll give her that. I swayed back and forth, thinking of another way to challenge Wyatt and Carlyle.

Then Zoe rolled backward and pointed at my rollerblades. "Those! Those are your answer!"

I glanced down, curling my toes inside my rollerblades. And then I smiled.

Friday. 5:45 PM. Skating rink DJ booth.

Zoe stood outside the DJ booth as I exited. The DJ was a cool guy, probably a junior or senior in high school, who also had a hint of a mustache. I told him that I was Chase Cooper, and that the whole song dedication was a joke to make me feel terrible. The best part was that he said he was really sorry and that if he knew it was a joke, he wouldn't have done it. But because of that, he agreed to help me out.

"What'd he say?" Zoe asked.

"Just have to wait 'til the end of this song," I replied. "Which gives me a few minutes."

"What until then?" she asked.

I looked around the skating rink and saw Faith in the dining area. I gulped, and started skating toward her. "There's something I have to take care of."

Friday. 5:46 PM. Skating rink dining area.

I rolled up to the table Faith was sitting at. It was the same table Zoe's friends were also at. "Hey," I said as smoothly as possible.

She looked up, embarrassed. "Hey."

I pointed at the speakers on the ceiling. "So you heard that song dedication, right?"

She nodded.

"You know that wasn't me," I said, rolling forward on my skates. The other girls at the table giggled a little.

"I figured," Faith said. "Whoever did it is a real jerk."

I nodded, feeling those butterflies dance in my stomach again.

This entire week had been one gigantic rollercoaster ride of emotions that left me feeling exhausted. I hated that Faith was dragged into this whole thing. She didn't deserve it – nobody did. I'd been fighting it this entire time, afraid of what everyone else was saying, but I realized tonight... who *cares* what other people think? Faith was awesome, and I needed for her to know that. Other than Zoe, she was the coolest girl I've ever met... and it was time for me to "man up."

I slapped my hands together and started feeling twitchy. "Well, the thing is... I wish it *was* me that dedicated that song."

The other girls at the table dropped their jaws.

Faith looked confused, blinking at me.

I started stretching my arms back and forth, I don't know why. Nervousness maybe? "I *wouldn't* have had the DJ say all that sappy stuff, but the *truth* is... I think you're cool. That note that was hung up this week—"

Emily pointed at the wall where a copy of my note was coincidentally hanging.

"Yes, *that* one, thank you," I groaned. "I wrote that note for real. I didn't mean for the entire *world* to see it, but I *did* want *you* to see it."

Faith blushed. I saw a grin split on her lips as she took a sip of her soda.

The speaker cracked from overhead, and the music changed, to a suspenseful tune played by an orchestra. The DJ spoke over the song. *"Laaaaaaadies and gentlemen! Boys and girls, we've just had our first skating rink challenge issued today!"*

Everyone in the skating rink slid to a stop and grew quiet.

"If all of you would be so kind as to leave the skate floor, we'll have our contestants ready themselves at the center of the rink."

Immediately, kids rolled through the space in the brick wall and off to the sides of the skating rink, squeezing themselves in where they could.

"Wyatt and Carlyle, would you enter the skate floor please!"

I watched as the leader of the red ninjas and the pirate captain reluctantly rolled onto the hard floor of the skating rink. The colorful overhead lights continued to blink on and off.

The two boys looked confused as they spoke to each other. They shrugged their shoulders as they looked at the group of spectators on the side of the skating rink.

The DJ continued. *"Chase Cooper, would you please join the other two contestants on the skate floor."*

"Chase?" Faith asked from her seat. "What's going on?"

I glanced over my shoulder. "I'm putting a stop to all this," I said boldly. "At least I *hope* I am."

I found my way through the crowd of kids until I came to the spot on the wall that was open. Putting my foot forward, I pushed off and rolled to the center of the rink.

When Wyatt and Carlyle saw me, they looked annoyed.

"What's this all about?" Wyatt asked.

Carlyle answered. "This scallywag means to

112

challenge us in some way, cousin."

I spoke quietly enough so only the two bullies could hear me. "I know it was the two of you who put copies of note up in the school."

"Of course you do," Wyatt said. "Because I *told* you it was us, like, two days ago."

I folded my arms, rolling circles around them, and then I spoke louder, so everyone in the rink could hear me. "What's that? You *don't* accept my challenge?"

The DJ in the booth played a sound effect of a baby crying.

Carlyle clenched his fists. "What's your *game*,

matey?"

Wyatt shouted at the spectators. "We never said we didn't accept the challenge! Whatever it is, we'll do it! We accept!"

That was the cue for the DJ in the booth to list the terms of the match. *"The challenge has been accepted!"*

The crowd slowly clapped, confused about what exactly it was they were applauding.

"The match is a race around the skating floor – first place out of three laps is the winner!"

"Another race, eh?" Carlyle asked, grinning. "I won't lose this time, son. A Norwegian obstacle course be one thing, but rollerskatin' be somethin' I'm quite skilled at."

"Good," I said. "So this should be easy for you."

"So what do I get if I win?" Wyatt asked.

I stopped, skidding my rollerblades on the ground. "Nothing except the satisfaction of beating me in front of everyone. And this time without the use of fists."

Wyatt glanced past me, at the kids of Buchanan. "And what do you get if *you* win?"

I smiled. "The same thing that you'd get."

"It's too late, you know," Wyatt added. "I've built another ninja clan, stronger than yours. The red ninjas have already risen to power behind the scenes. We're bigger than you think, and control more than you know."

"Maybe," I said, rolling backward. "But right now I'm only concerned about beating you in this race."

Wyatt made eye contact with his cousin, and

nodded. Carlyle smiled as he rolled on his skates to a line on the floor. I saw Zoe lean against the wall of the skating rink. Faith was right next to her, smiling so huge that the area around her actually looked brighter.

I wished that Brayden were there. I'll have to give him a call to let him know what happened.

"*Racers to your mark,*" said the DJ.

Rolling up to the line, I leaned forward, waiting for the DJ to start the race. Wyatt and Carlyle was standing right next to me, tapping their skates on the floor and taking deep breaths.

Over the speakers, the DJ spoke. "*On your mark...*"

I shut my eyes.

"*Get set...*"

Slowly, I exhaled, feeling my toes again in my rollerblades.

"*Go!*"

Immediately, I felt an elbow in my back. Then my face said hello to the floor. Carlyle had pushed me down!

The crowd shouted at Carlyle's sucker punch, but I couldn't let that stop me. I launched myself off the ground, and started running on my rollerblades. Without anyone else in the rink, I could swing my arms out without worrying about hitting anybody.

Wyatt took the lead with Carlyle right behind him. They were nearly twenty feet ahead of me, which doesn't sound like a lot but when you're only racing three laps around a small track, it's the same thing as being a hundred miles away.

Carlyle looked over his shoulder and laughed. "See ya!"

I rounded the first corner with ease, leaning my body into the turn and stepping my right foot over the left. As soon as I hit the straightaway again, I jumped forward with each push to gain as much speed as I could.

The DJ shouted over the speaker system. *"Off to a vicious start, Carlyle knocked Chase to the ground, but the ever determined Chase keeps pressing on!"*

I looked ahead of me. Wyatt was already on the other side of the track. My legs burned as I skated harder than I've ever skated in my life.

"Carlyle is racing strong, but it looks like Chase is catching up to him to – oh! And Chase passes Carlyle by the skin of his teeth!"

If the spectators cheered, I couldn't hear them. I was in the zone, like a ninja on rollerblades. If it were possible to catch fire, I think it would've happened.

"And Chase takes second place with ease at the start of the second lap! Wyatt still holding strong in the lead!"

Once I passed Carlyle, it was almost like he just gave up. He kept skating, but I flew ahead of him like it was nothing. Glancing to my left, I put my sights on Wyatt. I was gaining on him, but I wasn't there yet.

I saw Wyatt look over his shoulder at me. Once I rounded the turn again, I kept my head down and powered through. At this point, my thighs were killing me!

"It looks like Wyatt might've pushed too hard at the beginning folks, because Chase is catching up quickly at the start of the third and final lap!"

I rounded the second to the last corner, and saw Wyatt's shadow on the floor. He was close enough that I could smell his deodorant and hear his heavy breathing.

Once the path straightened again, we were neck and neck, throwing our arms and skating as hard as we could. Just one more corner and...

"Chase and Wyatt are in a dead heat, competing for the championship to... something! Chase pulls forward slightly as he takes the last corner. Wyatt swings out wide, but brings it back in, tightening the curve!"

I shut my eyes and gave it my all.

"Chase and Wyatt are side by side, givin' it everything they got and... and... it's a tie! They came in at a tie, folks!"

Wyatt cheered with his fists in the air. Carlyle skated to the side of the rink, clapping. Resting my hands on my knees, I let my skates roll to a stop. I felt irritated that I didn't dominate this race. Wyatt started skating to join Carlyle.

But the DJ kept talking. *"The race ends in a tie, but here at this skating rink, we don't allow ties. Chase and Wyatt to the center of the rink please for the tie breaker!"*

Catching my breath, I turned my skates and pointed them at the center of the rink. I looked at Zoe, but she shook her head, letting me know she had no idea what was happening. Faith was still next to her, clapping and shouting along with the other students.

"You should just give up now," Carlyle said as he sailed by me. "There's no way you'll win this. What's the tie breaker? Another silly race?"

"I don't know," I said honestly.

The speaker cackled, and the DJ's voice came through loud and clear. "*Shoot the Duck!*"

The entire skating rink exploded with cheers and screams of excitement.

Have you ever played Shoot the Duck? It's this insane game at skating rinks where everyone skates in a circle until the DJ says, "*Shoot the duck!*" Then everyone drops down and skates on one foot, while holding their other foot straight out in the front of them. You can't touch the ground with your hands or your other foot or you lose. You know what skill works best with this game? *Balance.*

Wyatt started skating around the track. I waited until he was on the opposite end before I started moving. The sound system had a wacky song playing over the speaker system.

As I rolled past the first turn, I kept my eyes on Wyatt. He was staring straight back at me. My legs were still shaking from the race, but some of it might've been because I was nervous. Balance wasn't one of my strong suits, and suddenly wished I had trained more with it.

I passed Zoe and Faith on the side. Over the shouts of other kids, I could hear them cheer me on.

And then it came.

"Shoot the duck!" yelled the DJ into the microphone. The music instantly shut off and the crowd grew silent.

I lowered my body slowly, and then stuck my left foot out. My muscles burned like someone hit them with a hammer! Keeping my foot off the ground, I rested my body on my bent leg, which is so much harder than it sounds! I wrapped my arms around both of my legs and hugged tightly, doing my best to keep balance.

Looking across the rink, I watched as Wyatt stuck his foot out too. He was using the same tactic of hugging his legs as I was – I guess ninjas think alike.

My foot started to wobble, and I brought my attention back to my extended leg. I didn't need to worry about Wyatt – I only had to focus on myself... and the powerfully ugly pain in my thighs! My legs! They were cramping! Another couple seconds, and I was going to be out of this contest!

Suddenly, the silence ended with a single scream followed by another eruption of cheers. When I looked over, Wyatt was laying on the floor of the skating rink, clutching his legs in pain.

"*Cramp!*" he screamed. "*Craaaaaamp!*"

I let myself drop to the ground and clutched at my own legs. I didn't want to say anything, but it hurt like crazy, and I screamed the same word Wyatt did. "*Craaaaamp!*"

"We have our winner!" the DJ said from his booth. "Chase Cooper has defeated Wyatt at Shoot the Duck! Make sure to congratulate him 'cause he's actually not going to receive a prize for it."

The students laughed. Zoe skated out and helped me to my feet. I did my best to stand, but my legs were trembling from pain.

The DJ spoke once more. "*Speech! Speech! Speech!*"

And the crowd joined in the chanting, slowly lowering their voices so they could hear me. I didn't want to give a speech! All I wanted to do was stop Wyatt and Carlyle from picking on me, and to do it *without* a fist!

"I think they want to you say something," Zoe said.

"You think?" I asked.

Thankfully, Wyatt broke the silence. "Why don't you marry Faith in front of all your new fans?"

I guess it was his way of being a sore loser, to tease me even *after* my victory, but honestly at that point, I truly didn't care. Wyatt on the ground, defeated. Carlyle

120

had lost in the first round so what did I care about the pirate?

But Wyatt kept going! "Why don't you give Faith a victory smooch!"

There were some kids who laughed at the suggestion, but not many.

I felt the pit of my stomach turn sour again, but then someone grabbed my hand. I jumped, surprised. It was Faith. She had skated out to the center of the rink to stand by my side.

Wyatt looked dumbfounded. I think he was trying to say something, but I couldn't understand anything coming out of his mouth.

Nobody else in the rink laughed with him anymore. Most of them had already moved on, skating circles on the track.

"Congrats," Faith said with a smile.

Embarrassed, I smiled. "Thanks. I uh... it was pretty difficult."

"I bet!" she replied.

I lifted our hands up. "So... does this mean...?"

Faith laughed and she squeezed my hand. "It means whatever it means."

I stared at her with my big stupid grin.

"Oh," Faith continued. "And we'll have no more of your sitting-alone-at-lunch nonsense. I was going to say something earlier this week, but you kept hanging out in the lobby. You're always welcome at my table with me and my friends."

It was kind of Faith to suggest, but I felt uncomfortable. "Thanks, but your table is full of girls, not that there's anything wrong with *that*, but I'd probably never hear the end of it."

Faith was confused. "What's there to make fun of? You'd be the *only dude* at a table *filled* with girls. Any guy at Buchanan would *kill* to have that spot."

I laughed, understanding she was totally right. But then I realized another thing – I didn't really care what anyone thought anyway, and that surprised me.

Gavin skated out to the center of the circle as his two hall monitors helped Wyatt off the rink.

"What's gonna happen to him?" I asked.

Gavin looked back at Wyatt. "Nothing, I suppose. We're not in school right now so my men are just helpin' him off the skate floor. As far as school goes, I'm not sure. There's not much evidence against him except for your word. It looks like he might get away with it."

As much as it pained me to think of Wyatt going unpunished, I realized something else – sometimes people get away with what they've done. It's unfair, but it *does* happen from time to time. All I could do was put best foot forward and leave it alone – try my best to "*play a different game*," as Zoe had said.

I took a breath, and asked, "What about the red ninja clan?"

"They're next on my agenda," Gavin said, "but I could use someone on my team who has experience."

I glanced at Faith, remembering that she knew my secret. "He means I'm a pretty good detective."

Gavin paused. "Right, if that's what you think I mean. Anyway, I'm sure that wasn't the last we seen of those red ninja fellas. Something tells me they'll be back."

"I think Chase will be a good addition to your team," Zoe added. "He's got special *skills* that make him an *expert* in that sort of thing."

I heard Wyatt shouting at the hall monitors to let him go once he was off the rink. I glanced over in time to see him swat the two boys off. "As long as *he's* at Buchanan, I think the red ninja clan is something we'll have to worry about." Then I looked at Faith. "But for tonight, I think I'm gonna just let it go."

She smiled at me.

Gavin nodded, and started skating away. "Alright

then. I'll see you first thing on Monday morning."

The lights to the skating rink switched off suddenly, and the disco ball lowered from a spot in the ceiling. A light hit it, reflecting thousands of dots across the floor. *"Moonlight skate for couples only,"* the DJ said with a low voice. *"Couples only, moonlight skate."*

I felt Faith let go of my hand as she started skating away. "Yeah, right," she laughed. "I wouldn't get caught *dead* skating the moonlight skate with someone!"

I laughed too, because it was a relief to not have to skate in the middle of the room while everyone was watching! I knew I still had a big dumb grin on my face as I caught up to her, but I didn't care. There wasn't anywhere else I'd rather be in that exact moment, and if I could make it last an eternity, I would.

It sounds sappy, I know, but guess what? I couldn't be happier.

Stories – what an incredible way to open one's mind to a fantastic world of adventure. It's my hope that this story has inspired you in some way, lighting a fire that maybe you didn't know you had. Keep that flame burning no matter what. It represents your sense of adventure and creativity, and that's something nobody can take from you. Thanks for reading! If you enjoyed this book, I ask that you help spread the word by sharing it or leaving an honest review!

- Marcus
m@MarcusEmerson.com

CHECK OUT THESE OTHER CRAZY-AWESOME BOOKS BY MARCUS EMERSON!

Marcus Emerson is the author of several highly imaginative children's books including the 6th Grade Ninja series, the Secret Agent 6th Grader, and Totes Sweet Hero. His goal is to create children's books that are engaging, funny, and inspirational for kids of all ages - even the adults who secretly never grew up.

Marcus Emerson is currently having the time of his life with his beautiful wife and their three amazing children. He still dreams of becoming an astronaut someday and walking on Mars.

Made in the USA
Middletown, DE
06 May 2021